I0553918

The Widows' Gallery

by

Marilyn Baron

The Lobster Cove Series

The Widows' Gallery

Cover Art by *Debbie Taylor*

The Wild Rose Press, Inc.
PO Box 708
Adams Basin, NY 14410-0708
Visit us at www.thewildrosepress.com

Publishing History
First *Last Rose of Summer* Edition, 2015
Print ISBN 978-1-62830-760-3
Digital ISBN 978-1-62830-761-0

The Lobster Cove Series
Published in the United States of America

Praise for Marilyn Baron

"Baron offers a bit of everything...humor, infidelity, murder, mayhem, and a neatly drawn conclusion."

~RT Book Reviews (4.5 Stars)

"I just finished reading *UNDER THE MOON GATE* and really enjoyed it. I was fascinated by the intertwining of the characters in the stories from the 1700s to present day and I especially enjoyed the segment that took place during WWII. Great writing. Marilyn did a great job of bringing Bermuda during the WWII era to life in this book."

~PJ Ausdenmore, The Romance Dish

"[*UNDER THE MOON GATE*] is a surefire blockbuster...a treasure trove of mystery and intrigue. It sparkles with romance... I couldn't recommend it more."

~Andrew Kirby

"An enjoyable read from start to finish...family, friends, enemies, intrigue and suspense...sadness, laughter, romance and ultimately love."

~Romance Junkies (4 Blue Ribbons)

"*SIXTH SENSE* has a great mix of romance, spine-tingling suspense, and real hope for two jaded individuals for a happily-ever-after ending."

~Tami Brothers

"An intriguing, albeit reluctant, psychic detective in this paranormal romantic suspense story...a strong and captivating heroine."

~Pauline Michael, Night Owl Romance (3 Stars)

Abigail Adams Longley looked around at the three women flanking her in Hall 10/14 of the Uffizi Gallery. They were all staring at *The Birth of Venus* like wide-eyed art students. Admittedly, the painting was as compelling as when the Medici family originally commissioned the tempera on canvas in the fifteenth century. But for Abigail, seeing the painting again wasn't cathartic. It was beautiful, but that wasn't the feeling she was going for. Peace. Why couldn't she get some goddamned peace in this life?

Abigail glanced at the square-cut, four-carat diamond on her finger, gazed at the sparkle of the ring she hadn't removed since the day Louis had proposed. And now, a whole year after his death, she still hadn't taken it off. Conventional wisdom dictated that you weren't supposed to make any major life decisions until a year after a spouse's death. Well, it had been a year already, and she hadn't wanted to make even one decision—major or minor—about where to live, where to go, or what to do. Whoever said money can't buy happiness had devised another dead-on axiom. She had all the money in the world—in fact Louis had left her a big chunk of the globe. He'd left her set for life, monetarily. But she would have traded every cent for the chance to be with him again. Louis was gone, and the sooner she faced the fact that she was alone on this planet, the better off she'd be.

Dedication

To Sandro Botticelli,
wherever you are in the universe,
thank you for painting *The Birth of Venus*,
my favorite work of art—
the masterpiece that inspired this story.
~*~

To my beautiful daughters Marissa and Amanda
(Venus has nothing on them),
my favorite living works of art.
~*~

To my husband, Steve,
who took me on a fortieth anniversary Mediterranean
cruise that started it all,
and to my dear friend and first reader,
Rae Stein, and her husband Barry,
who signed us up for the "free" cruise in Las Vegas
and who took the cruise with us.
~*~

And to my friend, Catherine Goetzke,
the best next door neighbor ever and book club buddy,
a voracious reader and an eternal inspiration.

Acknowledgments

To Abigail Adams Reynolds,
whose name I appropriated for my heroine, Abby.
She really was a descendant of John Adams,
the second President of the United States,
and was named after his wife, Abigail.
And for my good friend and neighbor,
Margee Kane,
for letting me do it.

Chapter One

Somewhere in the Mediterranean,
off the coast of Italy

There is a popular but anonymous Italian saying coined in the late 1700s, "See Naples and die!" Well, the cruise ship had just pulled away from Naples Harbor, and Victoria Dare was about to make that phrase a reality.

Victoria stared into the watery wake of the massive floating hotel. The superliner sliced through the water like a sharp knife through a hot buttered blueberry muffin. Weird she should think of food at a time like this. But she was going to miss blueberry muffins. And crispy bacon. And pancakes. And steaming hot chocolate, for that matter. Maybe it wasn't too late to change her mind and go to the dining room for one final breakfast—a Last Supper, of sorts.

And she would miss this fabulous view—so beautiful it was almost painful. The first rays of a rising sun warmed her face and caused her to squint. The surface of the water was smooth as glass, and it mirrored a calm she hadn't felt in a long time, as if there weren't a few thousand feet between the Lido deck and the ocean bottom. A place she was going to end up—she glanced at her watch—in five more minutes. Would her body sink to the depths of the ocean floor? Wash up on some picturesque Italian shore, her tender skin ripped to shreds by propeller blades? Or would she become shark bait?

She'd picked this secluded spot on the cruise ship for a reason. And this time—dawn—before the ship came to life. Victoria was nothing if not a planner. She'd planned her life down to the second, and now she was planning her own death in as structured a fashion. This was only a dry run. Victoria snorted. A dry run. She wouldn't be so dry when she finally took the plunge. Practice makes perfect. The motto reminded her of the marketing themes she created for her clients back in Atlanta.

But she'd recently resigned all her corporate marketing clients. The social media queen had become antisocial since her husband Zach's untimely death. Although when was death ever timely? She'd purchased a cemetery plot next to Zach's and had even written her own eulogy. She'd studied her death file in the stateroom before she emerged on deck, to see if she'd forgotten any last-minute details. Ever efficient, it seemed she'd taken care of everything. She'd traced her finger along the map outlining the ship's route and the stops along the way—Barcelona, Naples, Rome, Florence, Marseille, Palma de Majorca, and back to Barcelona. Well…she wouldn't be going back to Barcelona with the rest of the passengers.

Who would miss her if she disappeared into the watery void?

Her daughter, Emma, for one. And she was going to miss Emma terribly. They'd just spent some quality mother-daughter time in New York City, seeing the latest Broadway musicals, dining at their favorite Italian restaurants, wandering through museums. She'd even slipped in a final visit to the Fragonard Room at the Frick.

She'd miss hearing all about Emma's escapades with the online dating service—what Victoria now realized were her daughter's unsuccessful attempts to find her father, find a man who would take care of her, now that Zach was gone. She recalled their recent conversation over dinner when they'd discussed the fact that Emma was dating three men named Neil at the same time, after a disastrous breakup with a guy named Giuseppe.

"Isn't that Pinocchio's father?" Victoria had asked her daughter.

"Mom, that's Geppetto."

"Oh." Victoria had become quiet. She no longer believed in fairy tales.

Emma told her how she and Giuseppe had met. Giuseppe had texted her, "You're hot. Let's get together." Victoria couldn't believe her daughter wanted to meet a guy with such a cheesy pickup line. But since her father's death, Emma had been floundering and making bad decisions about men. The wrong kind of men. If she was trying to find The One, she was going about it the wrong way. It was obvious to Victoria what was happening, but she couldn't bring herself to verbalize it. She was in no position to criticize or counsel her daughter about happy endings or even provide comfort, when she was struggling to cope with her own loss.

Emma had agreed to meet Giuseppe, and it turned out he was hot, all right. In fact, he was steaming mad when, after several dates, he asked Emma back to his apartment and she said no.

"Do you remember what you wrote on your profile page?" he accused.

"I said a lot of things," Emma had replied.

"Under the number of dates it would take before you'd have sex, *you said* three to five," he reminded her. "This is our fifth date."

"It was just an estimate, not a guarantee," Emma had countered, adding, "Remind me to change that in my profile."

But Emma certainly wasn't going to miss her mother's annoying obsession with her love life or lack of one. It seemed doubtful Victoria was ever going to become a grandmother anytime soon, so, really, even at forty-something, this was the perfect time to go, before she became hopelessly attached to a precious new baby. Emma had a close circle of friends and a satisfying job in New York, so she'd be okay.

Victoria had purchased a beautiful green Italian inlaid burl-wood jewelry music box in Sorrento that played "Ritorno a Sorrento" when you lifted the lid. She'd placed her wedding ring in the box, had the store wrap it, and left a long letter on the package in her stateroom explaining her actions to her daughter. Though Victoria was pretty sure committing suicide was unexplainable.

Why was she doing it? Why snuff out her life? Because it was scary out there. And now she was single again. In the same boat as Emma. Well, not in a boat, exactly. On a humongous ship in the middle of the Mediterranean. Thousands of miles away from Emma. She was dying to call her daughter and listen to her sweet voice one last time, but she knew if she did she would lose her resolve.

And, if she jumped now, she'd miss seeing *The Birth of Venus* at the Uffizi Gallery on the excursion to Florence, the only item left on her bucket list. A chance to experience Sandro Botticelli's masterpiece once more in her lifetime. Returning to the gallery with Zach had been a dream of hers. But Zach was gone, and she didn't want to go on without him. Seeing the painting would bring back too many memories. A framed reproduction print of the painting hung over their bed. She had also chosen the classic scene as her desktop wallpaper and set it as her homepage. But she wanted to see the original again before she left this world. She reached for the picture of Zach she had just placed, carefully wrapped and protected, waterproofed, in the deep pocket of her jeans, and kissed it for the very last time. If there was an afterlife, and she believed it with all her heart, then, suicide aside, she would be seeing Zach again soon.

Victoria tensed in contemplation. What if they couldn't find each other in the hereafter? What if the fact that she had taken matters into her own hands, so to speak, prevented her from reaching Zach on the other side?

The last time she'd laid eyes on Botticelli's masterpiece was on her honeymoon. That first night in Florence, after visiting the Uffizi, a naked, engorged Zach, flexing his rippling muscles to tempt her in his imitation of *David*, was anxious to get down to business. He joked that the artist painted *The Birth of Venus* during his pagan phase. Victoria had been captivated by the peaceful sea-green colors, the golden tresses of the goddess, her ethereal beauty, and her modest yet sensual pose.

From the moment they'd first made love in the hotel room, Zach had called her his goddess of love. That painting represented the birth of their love. Seeing her favorite painting without Zach would be incomprehensible. But maybe she should delay her demise just a few more days. Then she could experience Rome again, and Palma de Majorca, a place she'd never visited.

"Vickie, you're nothing but a gutless coward. Just do it."

Victoria glanced around.

No one was out on deck yet. No sunbathers stirred. No walkers exercised, no joggers ran. Not a sign of the crew anywhere. She dragged over a chair and stood on it, teetering slightly as her hands clutched the ship's railing to steady herself.

Gingerly, she started to hoist herself up onto the railing—and ventured a look down. The distance to the water was farther than she'd thought. And she had calculated every aspect of her demise so carefully.

As she made her move, her body was jerked backwards, the chair tumbled, and she landed with a thud on the wooden deck.

"For God's sake! What are you doing? Are you trying to kill yourself?"

Victoria looked up at a statuesque woman, an angel in the mist. An angel with long, strawberry-blonde tresses that blew about her lovely porcelain face in the breeze.

It was Botticelli's Venus come to life. Only this Venus wasn't nude. She was dressed in a purple jogging suit.

Registering embarrassment, Victoria struggled to her feet, turned, and ran in the opposite direction.

"I was just practicing," she yelled over her shoulder.

Chapter Two

Florence, Italy

Abigail Adams Longley looked around at the three women flanking her in Hall 10/14 of the Uffizi Gallery. They were all staring at *The Birth of Venus* like wide-eyed art students. Admittedly, the painting was as compelling as when the Medici family originally commissioned the tempera on canvas in the fifteenth century. But for Abigail, seeing the painting again wasn't cathartic. It was beautiful, but that wasn't the feeling she was going for. Peace. Why couldn't she get some goddamned peace in this life?

Abigail glanced at the square-cut, four-carat diamond on her finger, gazed at the sparkle of the ring she hadn't removed since the day Louis had proposed. And now, a whole year after his death, she still hadn't taken it off. Conventional wisdom dictated that you weren't supposed to make any major life decisions until a year after a spouse's death. Well, it had been a year already, and she hadn't wanted to make even one decision—major or minor—about where to live, where to go, or what to do. Whoever said money can't buy happiness had devised another dead-on axiom. She had all the money in the world—in fact Louis had left her a big chunk of the globe. He'd left her set for life, monetarily. But she would have traded every cent for the chance to be with him again. Louis was gone, and the sooner she faced the fact that she was alone on this planet, the better off she'd be.

Abigail was named after the second First Lady of the United States, the wife of a distant relative, but what had she accomplished in her own lifetime? The name was a lot to live up to. And what had she contributed to the world? She burst into tears, and water poured like it was flowing from the Fountain of Neptune outside on the piazza. Shit. Shit. Shit.

A pretty woman next to her reached into her Furla bag. The same woman she'd pulled back from the brink of death on the Lido deck the other morning. She'd run away so fast Abigail hadn't had time to question her. She'd debated about reporting the incident to the captain, but then the woman had been in such a fragile state Abigail was afraid to tilt the balance, and apparently the woman had changed her mind, so who was she to interfere? Stiffening, the jumper implored Abigail with her eyes, pleading that she not mention what had happened, or had almost happened, that fateful morning.

"Here, take this," the woman said, extending a clean handkerchief she had pulled from her handbag. This Jennifer Aniston lookalike had purchased her new bag at the bottom of the Spanish Steps in Rome. These women were either stalking her or they had the same taste in leather goods, cruise excursions, and, apparently, in artwork. They had been on every excursion with her. First the city highlights tour in Barcelona, then to the farmhouse in Sorrento, next viewing Rome and the Vatican—an eternally arduous tour in the Eternal City. They didn't appear to know each other. Were they single, too? There was never any evidence of a man. Maybe their husbands were back on the ship, gambling.

She wished she could pretend Louis was just back on the ship. *I've got a little headache, Abby. Why don't you go into Florence? I wouldn't want you to miss "Venus on the Half Shell."* That's what she and Louis called *La Nascita di Venere*, a painting they both loved. That was where it had all begun for them. That's where she'd first met Louis. *The Birth of Venus* was the birth of their whirlwind courtship and romance. Abigail had been a student studying art history in Florence, Italy, and Louis had been on the Grand Tour, a college graduation present from his parents before he returned to Maine to go into the family business. As serendipity would have it, they were standing at the same time in the same place in the Uffizi Gallery, staring at the same painting—*The Birth of Venus*—when Louis looked at her and back to the painting and remarked, "You're the goddess in the picture. I didn't recognize you with your clothes on." He snapped her picture so he could "capture the moment they met."

Just one look was all it took for Louis. He told his Harvard friends to go on without him, and he stayed in Florence with Abby until she graduated. They traveled together throughout Europe, to every city in Italy and on to London, Amsterdam, Copenhagen, Paris, Madrid, Munich, and the Greek Islands. Then he brought her home to his parents in Lobster Cove and told them this was the girl he was going to marry. It had been a dream come true for Abby. They had been deliriously happy, totally devoted to each other, rarely spent a day apart until the very end, which had come much too soon.

They had everything—all the money in the world—and each other—and at the same time, nothing to leave behind. No children. No trace that Louis had existed in this world except the memory of how much she loved him.

Who was she kidding? Louis was not back on the ship. His little headaches had turned out to be a big brain tumor. A big, inoperable brain tumor. And one agonizing year later she was here, by herself, in a city meant for lovers, *without* one. And in her late thirties, who was ever going to love her again?

Revisiting her favorite city had seemed like a good idea when she booked the cruise. But whoever said "You can't go home again" was right. She didn't want to go back to Maine, to Longley House, that big mansion in Lobster Cove. Not alone. She hadn't really made friends in Lobster Cove. She hadn't even tried. There were only about 2,000 people who lived there. The population swelled to 2,500 during tourist season. She barely knew any of them, never associated with them. She and Louis had used Lobster Cove as a layover between international trips and business meetings. So now she was an outcast. She didn't belong. Maybe she could stay in Europe, perhaps settle in Switzerland or Italy, or France, or maybe England. She'd also considered buying a residence on a cruise ship and living there part-time—traveling to exciting destinations, enjoying gourmet dining and a world-class spa right outside her door. There was nothing for her back in the States. She was sick down to her soul, and so lonely it hurt. She needed something, but she couldn't articulate what that something was.

After dabbing her eyes, Abigail handed the

handkerchief back to the Jennifer Aniston lookalike.

"Keep it."

"Thanks," she sniffled.

The three other women turned to look at her, then the painting, then back to her.

"It's you," exclaimed one of them.

"What?"

"The painting. Venus. It could be you. Venus looks exactly like you."

"She could be your twin," agreed the second woman.

Louis had thought so, too. He'd called her his Venus. It was a compliment. The artist's model for *The Birth of Venus* must have been spectacular. Her long, blonde tresses, her chiseled face, her perfect body. A person could do worse than to look like the goddess of love and beauty. So she had accepted the compliment gracefully.

"Nice bag," Abigail commented, in an attempt to keep the conversation going. She'd been mumbling to herself or talking to Louis in her head for so long, it was nice to know her voice still worked.

"Thanks. I got it at—"

"Furla, I know. I got one too. I saw you there." She had seen the other women walking down the Spanish Steps, gazing forlornly at all the lovers—the couples kissing, wrapped around each other, or with his arm slung around her shoulder, happy, complete. And she had recognized their pain.

"Oh, were you on that excursion?"

"Yes. It was exhausting, wasn't it? I almost died when that tour guide walked us through the Coliseum in the hundred-degree heat. And then we did the Vatican tour. Fast-paced was an understatement. But nothing was worse than Stefano, our guide, force-marching us through Pompeii. I almost tripped on those cobblestones. I was definitely wearing the wrong shoes. Those petrified ash people looked better than I did."

"Jennifer"—or Furla Girl, as Abigail now designated her—looked at her and exposed a crooked, adorable smile. "I enjoyed it. And weren't you there at the farmhouse in Sorrento?"

"We all were. I loved the homemade olive oil and the mozzarella-tasting. I had some of their homemade honey shipped back to the States. And some bottles of wine. And I couldn't get over the size of those lemons. Although I would have preferred to spend the day in Capri, but that excursion was already booked up."

Suddenly energized, Abigail turned to the other women.

"Look, we've been traveling together for four days. I've seen you all over the ship, and we've had conversations during the excursions, so it's not as if we were strangers, but we've never been properly introduced. Do you ladies want to get a cappuccino or something out on the Piazza della Signoria and get to know each other better? My treat."

The three women standing shoulder to shoulder with her, eyes raptly fixed on the Botticelli masterpiece, shook themselves out of their trances, took one last longing gaze at Venus, sighed, and shrugged like they had nothing to lose. Like they'd already lost it all.

Abigail strolled out of the gallery and, after a brief hesitation, the women followed her one by one, like a line of obedient little ducklings, into the warmth of the Florentine sun.

"*Ciao, bella*," shouted one Italian man, dogging them from a safe distance. Italian men were harmlessly lecherous. They were basically cowards, at heart.

Abigail turned. A young man thought she was beautiful? Oh, probably he was catcalling to get Furla Girl's attention. She ventured a look at the catcaller. No, he was definitely ogling her. Probably hungering after her Sophia Loren body. Being in Italy was good for a fat girl's soul. Even the women in the paintings were curvaceous. Italian men liked voluptuous women, if she remembered correctly from her college days, when she'd spent those six months in Florence studying art history and Italian as part of a junior year abroad program. But she'd been younger then, and more appealing. And madly in love.

"*Signorina*?" The man was indefatigable.

"*Senora*," she corrected. Well, that wasn't right either. What was the Italian word for widow?

Here came the waterworks again. Maybe the women would think the noise and droplets were coming from the fountain across the cobblestones.

Furla Girl handed her another handkerchief. "Keep it. I won't be needing it."

Abigail gave her a quizzical look.

The women gathered at two tables under umbrellas at the Caffe Rivoire in the shadow of the statue of David. Not the real *David*. Abigail chuckled as she wondered how many clueless tourists had oohed and aahed over this David, and his most famous body part, leaving Florence without knowing this marble sculpture wasn't Michelangelo's *David*. The real McCoy had been moved from its original location in 1873 and was safely tucked away in the Accademia Gallery. This statue, delicious as it was to look at, was an imposter.

The waiter approached their table.

Abigail ordered in Italian. Why did she have to be such a fucking show-off? Her Italian was rusty, but these women didn't know that.

Furla Girl ordered a chocolate and a pastry—in English.

The woman next to her was wearing a chic Tadashi Shoji midnight-blue lace with Alexis Bittar earrings. She had that whole Jackie Kennedy mystique going on. Perfectly coiffed, rich sable brown hair, probably her crowning glory. No wedding ring. Looked to be near her own age, maybe about to hit the Big 4-0. She didn't look like a widow. What did a widow look like, anyway? Unlucky? "Jackie" ordered a cappuccino and biscotti.

Speaking of unlucky, Abigail had killed her lucky bamboo Louis had bought her just over a year ago. Instead of facing the reality that she was a plant killer and that everything around her was dying—including her in-laws in a plane crash, soon after Louis's death—she decided to ignore it and buy a new plant, as if the first one hadn't withered away from lack of attention. She was really going to try to take better care of the plant this time around.

Then the quiet one of the group ordered. The waiter had to bend down practically to her face to hear her. "*Cioccolata*," she whispered, and pointed to the raspberry layered cake with custard on the menu.

So the mouse knew a smattering of Italian, although she spoke it like a child. Impressive.

Abigail looked around the piazza and covered her head with a Memoire Vive scarf from Hermès. She loved to people-watch, but she could do without the aggressive pigeons.

She turned to Furla Girl. "Did you know that in classical antiquity the seashell Venus is standing on was a metaphor for a woman's vulva?"

Furla Girl choked on her water and crinkled her nose, Jennifer Aniston-style. "I wish you hadn't told me that. You've ruined the painting for me—and my appetite."

Abigail laughed.

"Did anyone ever tell you that you look like—?"

"Yes, Jennifer Aniston."

"Well, you do," Abigail said.

"I know, and what did that get me? My life still sucks."

Abigail blew out a breath. She didn't even know this chick, and yet she was intrigued. She felt a connection. She felt...protective of this unhappy kindred spirit.

"You don't have a corner on the 'shit happens' market," remarked "Jackie."

Furla Girl shook her head. "What's your problem?"

"How long do you have?"

Miss Mousey just sat there looking like she was about to dissolve into tears. Like she had just lost her best friend.

Way to break up a party, Abby. "Okay, ladies, we're in Florence, one of the most beautiful places in Italy—on earth, if you ask me. And all we can do is drown our sorrows? Let's celebrate."

"What's there to celebrate?" Furla Girl said, frowning.

Abigail looked pointedly at her. "We're alive."

The Jennifer Aniston lookalike let out a big laugh. And she wouldn't stop laughing.

"Inside joke?" "Jackie" asked.

Furla Girl paused. "The joke's on me. I can't do anything right. I can't even manage to kill myself, as one of you well knows. How hard is it to jump off a moving ship?" Then she gave the Neptune Fountain a run for its money.

Stupefied, Abigail turned to her and whispered, "You said you were just practicing. You weren't serious, were you?"

"Apparently not serious enough. I wasn't even supposed to be here."

Abby's heart melted. She had a new mission in life. Saving "Jennifer Aniston," aka Furla Girl. Whatever the hell her real name was.

"Okay, ladies, what's next on the agenda?" Abigail asked, in her new role as self-appointed take-charge director of this private tour. Louis always thought it best to face uncomfortable issues head on. She looked at Furla Girl.

"What are you going to do when you get back to the ship, besides take a swan dive off your balcony?"

The women at the table were silent. Furla Girl mopped her eyes and frowned.

So Abigail said, "I'm registered for the art auction at the gallery on the ship. I saw a Picasso I'm interested in bidding on."

Miss Mousey's eyes bulged. Abigail knew what she was thinking. What they all were thinking: How could this woman afford a Picasso? Well, it just so happened she could afford a roomful of Picassos, if she wanted to. Hell, she could buy them each a Picasso and it wouldn't make a dent in her bank account, which she was depleting at an express-train rate. But much as she tried, the damn thing kept growing. Apparently she had a money manager who was a genius.

"Of course, I'm just kidding," Abigail said, trying to lighten the mood. "We can check out the gallery, relax, enjoy some free champagne, just have some fun."

This crew didn't look like they knew the meaning of the word. They ate the rest of their food in silence, each lost in her own thoughts even as they headed for the pickup spot and Francesca, the tour guide, who was holding an orange umbrella above her head.

"You ladies have plans for dinner?" Abigail tried again.

"No," said Furla Girl.

"Well, would you like some company?" Abigail asked.

"I guess," the woman responded.

"How about you?" Abigail asked, looking at "Jackie."

"I'm free."

"And you?" Abigail asked Miss Mousey.

"No plans."

"It's a date, then. I'll make us all a reservation at the Italian specialty restaurant. The food is great, a step above the regular dining room. I've already eaten there twice."

"But doesn't that cost extra?" Miss Mousey asked.

"Thirty-five dollars, but, hey, it's my treat," said Abigail. "For all of you. I'm Abigail, Abigail Adams Longley, by the way."

"Like the wife of the second president?" Miss Mousey's eyes widened.

"I'm related to her husband, somewhere back in time."

"Seriously? That's amazing. I'm Natalie," said "Jackie." "Natalie Jasper."

Yes, that fits, Abigail thought. Jackie Kennedy, Natalie Wood. That dark, brooding classic beauty. Abigail wondered what her story was. She was curious about people. Just not the people back in Lobster Cove.

Abigail turned to the woman with the Furla bag as if they had just met. "What about you? What's your name?"

"Victoria," she said. "But my friends call me Vickie."

"Nice to meet you, Vickie."

All three turned to Miss Mousey, who blushed.

That girl is a librarian if there ever was one, Abigail mused. "Let me guess. Is it Marian?" No one laughed. No one got the reference to "Marian the Librarian" from *The Music Man.*

"No, it's Jane," she said. "Jane Nash."

Plain Jane. No, she wasn't exactly plain. Hard to tell her age. She was tiny, so maybe in her late twenties, but the way she dressed, so prim and proper, she might be closer to thirty-five. She could be pretty, but the way she covered up her figure, wearing no makeup, hiding those gorgeous blue eyes behind those serious tortoiseshell frames, who could tell? She was hiding out in there. She wasn't mousey. She was miserable. Her grief was fresh. And it was etched all over her face.

Marilyn Baron

Chapter Three

The waiter at Lucca's, the onboard Italian specialty restaurant, filled their crystal goblets with water and began flirting with the women at the table, upholding the reputation of Italian men everywhere.

"How about some wine?" Abigail suggested, noting that the waiter's Italian accent was affected, but she was too bored to call him on it.

"None for me," Jane said. Jane was on the bony side. She was probably wearing her nicest cocktail dress, but the total effect was just sad.

"Nonsense," Abigail insisted. "You're on a Mediterranean cruise. Do you prefer red or white?"

"Either is fine. Whatever you're having. I, uh, I'm not sure I drink wine."

Abby tried not to register shock. "You're not sure? Have you ever had wine before?"

Jane shook her head.

"She will have a glass of Zinfandel," said Abigail decisively, attracting the waiter's attention. "What about the rest of you? Come on, now, this is a celebration."

"What are we celebrating again?" asked Vickie.

"Our friendship." Abigail ordered a bottle of red and a bottle of white for the table. She studied the menu. The waiter stood poised to take their food orders.

"I'll have the spaghetti carbonara," Abigail

20

announced.

"Excellent choice," said the waiter, nodding and writing down her order.

The women each made a selection from the menu. Victoria went for the sea bass. Natalie chose shrimp scampi, and Jane went for plain spaghetti and tomato sauce. No meat or meatballs to spice it up. No sense of adventure.

When the waiter returned with the wine and poured it into her goblet, Abby swirled the liquid in her glass and took a whiff, followed by a small sip. She nodded appreciatively. He filled the other goblets on the table.

"Come on, you don't think it was an accident that we met, do you?" Abby posed. "We've all been on the same excursions since we set sail from Barcelona. I'd be willing to bet that if we compared notes, we've all chosen the same excursions for the rest of the cruise. We probably have a lot in common. We were meant to meet—for a reason."

"You believe in fate?" Vickie wanted to know.

"Of course," answered Abby.

Natalie picked up her wine glass. "What reason could there possibly be?"

"I don't know, but I think we owe it to ourselves to find out," Abby stated. "Now, maybe I'm getting too personal, but are there any husbands in the picture? Are you married, single, divorced?" Abigail paused and swallowed the lump threatening to form in her throat. "Widowed?"

"I'm recently widowed," Natalie explained.

"Me, too," responded Abby. "How recently?"

"Five years."

"Five years?" Abby blanched. "I'm only one year

out. Is this what I have to look forward to?"

"Howard was a wonderful man," whispered Natalie. "He was irreplaceable. I mean, he wasn't perfect, by any means, but I never really appreciated him until he was gone."

"I'll never get over my Zach," echoed Vickie.

"Louis was a dream husband," Abigail agreed. "I'll never find another man like him." She imagined it was the same for all widows. They tended to forget the bad things and only remember the good. Husbands couldn't all be saints, but Louis had come pretty close. He had to be a saint to put up with her snarkiness.

Abigail turned to Jane. "What about you, Jane?"

Jane whimpered and then exploded into sobs. Each of her tablemates offered a tissue to the woman in distress.

"Get ready for some table drama," Abby whispered to Vickie.

Jane wiped her eyes on her cloth napkin.

"This was supposed to be our honeymoon cruise." Other restaurant patrons stared at the table while Jane struggled to regain her composure.

"That stinks," said Abby. *And it explains a lot.*

"We never even made—" Jane downed her glass of wine and hiccupped. "Love."

The three others looked at each other to avoid looking at Jane.

"That's right, I'm still a virgin," stated Jane. "I'll have another glass of wine, please."

Abigail filled Jane's wine glass. "Why didn't you cancel the cruise?"

"It was too late to get our deposit back."

Abby surveyed the group. "Any kids?"

"One daughter—Emma," announced Vickie. "She's the most beautiful girl, my pride and joy. And my best friend."

Abigail frowned. "You have a daughter, and you were going to drown yourself?"

Victoria nodded sullenly. The other women were too shocked to speak.

"Louis and I tried, but we were not blessed with children. We wanted three. We already had names picked out. Louis was into the stock market. We were going to call them DAX, after the German index, if it was a boy; DJIA, the abbreviation for the Dow Jones Industrial Average, for a girl or a boy; and CAC or Catherine, after the CAC 40, the benchmark French stock market index, if it was a girl."

Abigail turned to Vickie. "If I'd had a child, I would never leave her alone on this earth, not on purpose."

Victoria fixed Abigail with a lethal glare. "You don't know what you'd do. Grief can really mess with a person's mind."

"I know all about grief," Abby protested.

"Apparently you know all about everything," Victoria said snidely. "Suddenly, I feel very tired. I'm going back to my cabin."

Abigail grabbed Victoria's arm. "To kill yourself? Are we going to wake up tomorrow morning and find out about a bereft female passenger who jumped overboard in the middle of the night, and then we'll have to turn the ship around and look for your bloated body in the middle of the Mediterranean and miss the rest of our excursions?"

Victoria pulled her arm back. "I'd hate to

inconvenience you."

"That's not what I meant. What I meant was, I'm not—" Abigail looked around. "*We're* not—going to let you do it. You are going to bunk in my suite tonight, or we're going to stay up all night. We're not going to let you out of our sight until you straighten yourself out."

"You make it sound like I have a bad back or a muscle spasm. My husband is dead. I don't care about living anymore."

By now everyone in the restaurant was staring at them.

"Besides, I don't even know you," Victoria railed. "Why do you care if I live or die?"

"Because I *am* you. I've been there, right where you are. I'll wager we all have. And life is too precious to throw away." When did she become so philosophical?

Victoria gripped her chair and gritted her teeth.

"Ladies," Abigail said. "Victoria's right. We don't know each other, but I think we need each other. For instance, what are you doing with the rest of your lives?"

"I owned a marketing firm, but I've resigned all my clients, tied up all my loose ends," Victoria admitted.

"I'm in corporate real estate," said Natalie. "In upstate New York. Not much action in the market, and I can't stand the winters. I'm thinking of moving."

"What about you, Jane?" Abigail asked.

Jane took another sip of wine. By now she was gulping it down like Kool-Aid.

"I'm an artist."

Abigail's eyes lit up. "Would I have seen anything

you did?"

"Probably not. I'm not very well known."

"What kind of things do you paint?"

"Mostly landscapes and seascapes," said Jane. "I love the ocean. This is the first time I've seen it."

Abby's jaw dropped, shocked when she contemplated Jane's sheltered existence.

"Do you have a Web site?" asked Victoria. "Because if you don't, I can set one up for you."

"Before or after you abandon ship?" Abigail remarked dryly.

"Shut up."

"I-I do have a Web site," Jane admitted.

"Well, let's see it. Do you have an iPhone?"

"No," said Jane apologetically. "And you can't get service on the ship unless you go to the Internet café."

"Yes, you can. There's wireless on the ship. You have to pay for it, but—" Abigail caught herself. She could afford the exorbitant fees the ship charged. Jane obviously couldn't.

"I have some cards with my work on them," Jane said.

"Hand them over," Abigail demanded.

Jane opened her handbag, one which was entirely inappropriate for a dressy dinner. It didn't even match her dress. It wasn't even real leather. The poor girl probably didn't own a proper evening bag. She probably didn't have a penny to her name. On their way out of the restaurant, Abigail decided, she would buy Jane a nice evening bag in one of the onboard shops, something glitzy and frivolous, with Swarovski® crystals—or gift her with the new Furla bag she had just purchased in Rome. She could always buy another one.

She had a closetful of handbags. More than one Furla bag. More than she needed. More than she could ever use in a lifetime.

"Here," said Jane, thrusting a handful of postcards into Abigail's waiting hands. Abby spent about a minute studying the cards. This girl had some serious talent.

"Holy shit, Jane. You're actually good. No, better than good. Everyone, look at this. Jane is a budding Chagall." Abigail passed the cards around the table. "And look at this one—more like Monet than Monet."

"I'm nowhere near that good," Jane protested shyly.

"You've been hiding your light under a bushel, as my grandmother used to say," Abigail disagreed. "Who represents you?"

"Nobody."

"Where do you live?" Abigail put down her wine glass.

"North Dakota."

"Don't they have art galleries in North Dakota?"

"Not in my town."

"Jane, Abigail's right," said Natalie. "Your work is fantastic. The colors are so vibrant. I love your style. You paint in the style of Chagall, but you're an original."

"Are these for sale?" asked Victoria. "Because I want to buy one. I'm an artist myself in my spare time, but this—I mean, you paint on a higher level."

"I can give you a painting."

"Jane, you don't just give away your work," Abigail snapped. "Where's your self-respect? Well, you've obviously got talent. Victoria is a marketing guru. And Natalie can sell the hell out of a house."

"Business," corrected Natalie. "Sell the hell out of a business. And what about you? What talent do you have?"

"Money," Abigail answered and smiled. "Lots and lots of money. Listen up. I'm beginning to get an idea. What brought us together in the first place? What do we all have in common?"

Abigail was greeted with puzzled looks.

"Art! We were all drooling over *The Birth of Venus*. We spent hours wandering around the Uffizi Gallery, gawking at the masterpieces. Jane is one of the most talented artists I've ever seen. And I've been all over the world. We're all at a place in our lives where we need a change. What if we opened an art gallery?"

Victoria's eyes brightened. "Are you serious?"

"Dead serious."

The irony wasn't lost on Victoria. "Enough with the dead jokes, Abigail. I'm not going anywhere. But where would we locate the gallery? I mean, I live in Georgia. Natalie is in New York. Jane is in North Dakota, for heaven's sake. Where do you live, Abigail?"

"In Maine, in a small town near Bar Harbor, right on the Atlantic. It's called Lobster Cove."

"I've always wanted to live on the ocean," said Jane, a longing look in her eyes.

"Do any of you have any commitments, leases, house payments, anything?"

"All my affairs are in order," reported Victoria.

"I'm ready to move at a moment's notice," offered Natalie.

"I was renting an apartment, and the lease is up.

After the honeymoon I was going to move onto Jimmy's farm. Well, he doesn't actually own it. We were going to move into his parents' house. But now, I guess I'm homeless."

Abigail beamed. "Not anymore. I have this monstrous mansion—with some great ocean views—in Lobster Cove. I'm rambling around all alone in there, and I'm desperate for company. The house even comes with a French chef, courtesy of my dead in-laws."

"But what do any of us know about running an art gallery?" Victoria asked, and the others nodded and looked questioningly at Abigail.

"Natalie, the way you're dressed, you obviously have style to spare. With the help of an architect, you could help me transform the interior space and customize it for the gallery. Victoria, you could market us. I'll finance our venture. And Jane will be our first featured artist."

"Where would we get the other paintings?" asked Victoria.

Abigail swept the room with her hands. "We're in Europe, ladies. When the ship docks back in Barcelona, we're going on a treasure hunt. First in Spain. Then the rest of the continent. There are thousands of artists all around Europe—and in the States. While we're over here we can stop in Prague, talk with some artists on the Charles Bridge, visit Montmartre in Paris. There is some fabulous undiscovered talent in Yugoslavia, and, of course, let's not forget Italy."

"But I can't afford to stay in Europe even one more day." Jane sighed. "I'm on a strict budget."

"Jane, I have a boatload of money I don't know what to do with. Don't worry about the cost. I have a feeling this is going to be a great investment."

Victoria's face lit up. "Do you really think this could happen? We have a lot of things to work out. What if we fail? "

"Louis always said, 'Failure is not an option,' " said Abigail. "And you can't succeed if you don't try. We can work out the details. But we can't do it without you, Vickie. So you have to promise not to off yourself."

Victoria blushed.

"Are we all in?" Abigail asked. "How about a toast to our new gallery? Wait! What are we going to call it?"

"We could name it after the ship," Jane suggested.

"The Ligurian Queen?" Abigail snorted. "Sounds like a Humphrey Bogart classic."

"What about the Florence Gallery," said Natalie, "the city where we all met?"

"No, that doesn't have the right ring to it," Abigail said.

"How about Botticelli's?" Vickie offered.

"Sounds too much like an Italian restaurant," said Abigail. "But I like the sound of it. It's close."

"What about the Widows' Gallery?" said Jane, pouring herself another glass of wine.

"Appropriate, but too maudlin," argued Natalie.

"I know," Vickie said. "We all love *The Birth of Venus*. That painting brought us together. How about the Venus Gallery?"

The women screamed in unison. By now everyone in the restaurant was riveted on their conversation.

"That's it," Abigail squealed and raised her glass. "That's perfect. We're all beautiful, intelligent women.

Venus and Aphrodite were the Roman and Greek goddesses of love, beauty, prosperity, and sex." Abigail looked at Jane. "Well, some of us have had sex. I can't think of a better name for our new venture. This calls for a toast. Let's drink to the success of the Venus Gallery."

Chapter Four

Lobster Cove, Maine
Three Months Later

Abby stormed out of the house like a hurricane headed for open water while her mind spun out of control. She needed a break. She grabbed her purse, ran down the hill, and headed into town to the Lobster Cove Post Office. And woe to anyone who so much as tried to approach her, talk to her, or get in her way.

She glanced at her watch. One thing she hated was being kept waiting. And that ditzy-sounding Valdosta McKinley had been a no-show at the interview for the Venus Gallery manager position. She'd had the chef prepare a marvelous lunch for Miss No Respect For Anyone's Time But Her Own, and when the ungrateful twit didn't keep her appointment, Abby was furious, starving, and pissed. With their horrendous schedule to open this art gallery, she didn't have a nanosecond to spare. If that little snit from Nowhere, West Virginia, thought she was going to get a job as the gallery manager, she had another think coming. And what kind of name is Valdosta anyway? Who names their child after a city? Well, besides Paris Hilton, that is. And that Southern accent she'd originally thought quaint was probably fake. Of course, she'd called about a half hour later saying she knew she was expected at ten, but

Abby didn't give her time to explain herself. She asked Valdosta—or Val, as she preferred to be called—if she made a habit of being rude and unreliable, and Val denied it. Miss Undependable asked if she could reschedule, and Abby had hung up on her. A manager late to her own appointment? And she had sounded so organized on the phone. The woman had credentials out the wazoo, but that was all on paper. She obviously had no work ethic. And that was a death knell when dealing with a demanding woman who was ultra-impatient.

She'd told the chef to serve lunch to her friends in the dining room as a special treat. If the interview went well, she'd be introducing them to the new gallery manager. But she was so incensed she couldn't risk facing the others. They'd probably already surmised that she was a bitch, and Abby didn't want to confirm their suspicions. She wanted to get out of the mansion, away from the constant clanging, buzzing, hammering, and drilling going on in the gallery space. She knew Jane would be up in her newly converted third-floor loft, painting her heart out. The girl hadn't put down her paintbrush since she'd arrived, she was so enthralled with the fucking view. A view Abby had obviously taken for granted all the years she'd lived in Lobster Cove. You'd think the girl had never seen an ocean before. Well, of course she hadn't, not until their cruise. But she was obsessed with the ocean view from her new studio—and obsessed, too, with that quiet but attractive Southern charmer, Ethan Logan, an artist they'd discovered and recruited on one of their art acquisition trips, the one to Charleston, South Carolina. He'd arrived on the scene to deliver some of his paintings, and Plain Jane was coming out of her shell.

And Natalie was enclosed (and maybe declothed) with the architect, that hunky Aidan Ames, from Ames & Associates. They spent most of their days huddled over blueprints, picking out colors and materials. Natalie was mad for the guy, and who could blame her? Pheromones as thick as dust mites were flying all over the construction site, streaking on the sunlight, invading the atmosphere. Apparently Natalie had choked on them.

At least Victoria wasn't affected. She'd hardly taken a break from her computer. She and that machine were joined at the hip, but she was doing a fantastic job with the gallery promotion. They were only a month away from the opening. And they were behind in every way you could be behind.

Their whirlwind buying trip around Europe had been an unqualified success. They had found amazing paintings, drawings, furniture, and decorative arts to complement the artwork they'd collected from around the continent. This was going to be the most impressive private gallery on the planet. She was proud of all the work they'd done, but it wasn't enough. And now that little witch of a would-be gallery manager had gone and wasted two, count them, *two* full hours of her precious time. Two unrecoverable hours. And now she was wasting more valuable minutes thinking about her.

The prize painting they'd snagged from a Berlin art dealer, a Botticelli, *Portrait of Venus*, was one of the holdups. It had cost her a fortune, literally, and it was slated to be the main attraction for the gallery. But just yesterday a representative from a London-based international task force, a European art theft organization, which operated the Lost Art Database

Web site, had called, claiming it belonged to a Jewish family and had been sold under duress during World War II. Vickie had gone ballistic, and her side of the telephone screaming matches must have been audible all the way into town. The lawyer—also a renowned art historian—who had traced the painting's provenance, had promised to arrive in Lobster Cove to authenticate the painting and show Victoria the documents to prove the dubious history. And after Vickie showed him her papers refuting his claims, she was going to show him the door.

Abby was still agitated as her clogs click-clacked on the wooden dock, heading toward Longley House and away from the Lobster Cove Post Office, where she had just opened a business post office box for the Venus Gallery. She was examining her brand-new key when she felt a thud and the breath left her body. She had rammed into something hard, knocking her head against the impediment with a jolt. Her legs turned to jelly, and she literally saw stars. Tripping over her wedges, she started to topple, flailed and reached out, windmilling, as she flew through the air, hoping not to fall into the water.

Strong arms enveloped her and stopped her forward trajectory.

"You need to watch where you're going, lady," a brusque voice barked.

Abigail looked up, and her eyes widened at the giant standing there. She was still wrapped in his arms, caught like a rabbit in an embrace as tight as a steel trap. She tried to wriggle out of his grip. The man was built like a Volvo truck, and he had all the grace of the fishermen who lived in the town. She stared up at his hard body and into his face, which though gruff was painted with concern.

Her heart stuttered, her pulse quickened, and she felt an instant attraction. Christ, the man was gorgeous—and a little dangerous-looking—with a possible hint of Native American going on against the rugged planes and angles of his chiseled face. And that body! My God, it was positively Olympian. She couldn't look away or change the goofy smile she felt spreading across her face.

"Me?" she seethed. "You plowed right into me, you big, clumsy oaf." Steadying herself in his embrace, she gazed up into the deepest blue eyes she'd ever seen. Eyes as relentless as the ocean.

The giant shook his head. "I saved you from drowning, or at least a concussion. You were going over and under, sweetheart."

"Don't call me sweetheart, buster," Abigail warned.

A hint of a smile appeared on the man's face. "Buster?"

Goliath set her on her feet and held her by the elbows to steady her.

Abigail took a step back to study him more closely. Her eyes focused on his overalls. He was probably a blueberry farmer. There were a lot of those in Maine. Or a cranberry farmer, like those two dweebs in the juice commercial, wading in the water in their hip-high rubber boots. Or a dock worker. Or a fisherman. Or someone who had come over to this country in steerage. No doubt some kind of laborer.

"Hey, you'd better sit down. Are you hurt?"

Abigail dusted herself off. "Just feeling a little

dizzy." She clutched her key.

"What's that in your hand?"

"That is a key to our new P.O. box."

"Why do you need a P.O. box?"

"Not that it's any of your business, but it's for my new gallery. We're opening in a month."

"A gallery? You mean like an art gallery?"

"No, a shooting gallery." She snorted.

"Maybe you're hungry or dehydrated. Let me buy you lunch until you settle," said the titan.

"I don't have time, and anyway, I don't even know you," she said.

"I'm Tack. Tack Garrity."

"What kind of name is Tack?"

"Apparently you don't sail," noted Tack. "It's a family name that dates back to the 1880s. One of my ancestors was the captain of a whaling ship. Say you'll let me buy you lunch. I was headed over to Mariner's Fish Fry. It's a bit upscale, but it won't break the bank."

"Chef is preparing lunch."

"You have a chef?"

"I've got to eat, don't I?"

"I assume he's French."

"Of course. What's Mariner's Fish Fry?"

"You must be new here. Come to think of it, I haven't seen you in town. Surely, if you lived here, you'd have been to Mariner's Fish Fry. It's a diner/restaurant, one of the best in town for fresh lobster and lobster rolls, and they always feature a great catch of the day. They have a new lobster fritter on the menu as an appetizer. On the northern end of the harbor. The place has been here for decades."

"No, I'm not familiar with that *establishment*,"

Abigail admitted, accenting the last word with disdain. "Don't worry about me. I'm just a little dizzy."

He rubbed her arms.

"You can let me go now." But she really didn't want him to.

The giant's face reddened as he started to release Abigail.

"I've told you my name. What's yours?"

Abigail hesitated. "Abigail Adams...Longley."

"As in *the* Longleys? You were Louis's wife?"

Abigail's eyes widened. "Did you know Louis?"

"We didn't exactly hang out in the same circles, but yes, I knew him. I went to public school. He went to prep school. I was sorry to hear about Louis's death and your in-laws being killed in that plane crash right after they lost their son. That must have been rough. You got a raw deal."

"It hasn't been a picnic."

Abigail studied Tack. The man was nothing like Louis. Louis had been slight of build, quiet, unassuming, bespectacled, and brilliant. She resented this man *because* he wasn't Louis and yet he was making her feel things she hadn't felt, well, since she'd lost Louis.

"Look, I'm really sorry," said Tack. "Are you okay? Your face looks—I mean, I think you landed pretty hard against my stomach."

You mean your rock solid abs? Abby tried to calm her heart and catch her breath.

"I wasn't watching where I was going," Tack apologized, after depositing her lightly onto the wooden walkway. "I had a lot of things on my mind, and I was distracted."

Abby knew she hadn't been watching where she was going either, but she wasn't about to admit it.

"Well, you should pay more attention next time," Abby admonished.

Tack smiled. "So. You live up there in the Longley mansion?"

"Yes."

"All alone?"

"Well, not anymore. Some friends are living with me. We're opening the gallery together."

Tack looked at his watch. "Look, I'm late. I'm going to meet my daughter. Why don't you have lunch with us? It won't take long. Just until you calm down."

Abby wondered if Tack could hear her stomach growling. She was hungry enough to eat a raw fish with the head on, and she hated sushi. In her current mood, she wasn't going to get much done today. And he hadn't been completely at fault when he ran into her. What harm could it do to have lunch with this hayseed blueberry farmer? She loved blueberries.

"Okay, thank you." She tried to sound gracious, but gracious wasn't really part of her repertoire.

Tack placed a broad hand on her shoulder and aimed her toward the restaurant. She stared at his hand.

"I just want to make sure you don't fall again, not on my watch."

Tack took her by the hand and led her toward Mariner's Fish Fry, the blue and white building ahead, with its green canopy over the entrance, a canopy emblazoned with a large red lobster. To the left of the building was a short, squatty, non-operational lighthouse with a deck circling the second floor. The place had a definite harbor flavor.

Abigail's hand tingled where Tack touched it. For such a big man, he had a surprisingly light touch. Or maybe she was just super sensitive. It had been awhile since a man had touched her.

"We've got to hurry. My mom dropped my daughter off, and I was already running late. Look, I apologize for running into you. I just finished a cruise, and we didn't spot even one whale, so I had to refund half the ticket price to every passenger. That's a half a day shot. I hate to lose the money, but more, I hate that the tourists were disappointed."

"What do you do?"

"I'm the captain of Lobster Cove Adventure Cruises. It's a whale-watching tour. I dock north of town and pick up and deliver passengers to Pier 2, the general pier here in town. We sail along the coast, and the passengers get to see nature—puffins to their heart's content, and sometimes whales. But today I took her out almost to Canada, and still no whales."

"So, you'll make it up tomorrow," Abigail said.

"It's not the first time this has happened. At this rate, I'm going to lose the boat, and that's going to break my dad's heart."

"What's your dad have to do with it?"

"It's his boat. We had to put him in Rutherford's. That's a nursing home on the outskirts of town. I moved back from Boston to take over."

"How did you know how to do it? Captain a boat, I mean."

"I used to go out with my dad all the time."

"So now you spend all day watching whales?"

"It's more than that— Excuse me." Tack bounded into the restaurant and up to the hostess station, where he took the hostess in his arms and twirled her around.

"Dawn, is Isabella here yet?"

"At your usual table, Tack. Don't worry. I've been keeping a good eye on her."

"Thanks. Dawn Sullivan, this is Abigail Longley. Dawn and her husband, Roark, own this place."

"I don't believe we've ever had a Longley in here," Dawn assessed acerbically. "Well, there's a first time for everything."

"I don't think she likes me," whispered Abigail, as Tack led her toward a large booth by the window at the back of the restaurant. Some diners were seated on the back deck at picnic tables that overlooked the bay.

"That's just her way." Tack leaned down and scooped his daughter up in his arms.

"Daddy!" The girl's grin spread from ear to ear. She wound her arms around his shoulders and offered him a kiss.

"Isabella, this is Abigail."

Isabella stood up and announced, "I'm Queen Isabella, and I'm going to marry the Prince of Whales."

Abigail laughed and curtsied. "Your Highness," she said before turning to Tack. "So she's set her sights on the Prince of Wales. Does she know he's already taken?"

"Not that Prince of Wales. The Prince of Whales, the mammal variety."

"Oh, I see."

"Isabella, scoot over so Miss Abigail has some room."

Abigail stared at Isabella. What a beautiful child. Her heart melted. *This could have been my child.*

Isabella's ice-blonde hair fell in ringlets around her

head. Dressed in a beautiful silver-embroidered turquoise tulle tutu and a tiara, she looked like a fairy princess—except the tutu was on inside out.

Abby looked at Tack. "Queen Isabella?"

"Her mother used to call her that."

That revelation posed some questions. Was Isabella's mother out of the picture? And if so, were they divorced? Or was theirs a great love story?

"Did you order for us, Princess?"

"It's *Queen* Isabella, Daddy."

"Of course. Forgive me. I seem to be apologizing to women all over the place today."

So the blueberry farmer had a sense of humor.

"Daddy always orders the same thing. A lobster roll, mashed potatoes, and green beans." Isabella turned to Abby. "What are you having?"

"That sounds good. I think I'll have what your Daddy's having."

The server came over and started to hand Abby a menu. She looked to be in her early twenties.

Tack intercepted the menu and handed it back to the server, planting a kiss on her cheek. "Katelyn, she'll have what I'm having. Thanks. And Abigail, what will you have to drink?"

"I'd love a lemonade if you have it." Although she was dying for something stronger.

"Coming right up." The server filled their water glasses, then left to put in their food order.

"You're on a first-name basis with the waitress? You sure are a friendly sort."

"Sure. Katelyn Sullivan is the owner's daughter. I can't believe you've never eaten here."

Abby stared at the displays of old wooden lobster

traps, nets, and lobster buoys on the wall. "I thought it was just a hangout for fishermen and such." She probably sounded like a real first-class snob. "Besides, I don't spend much time in Lobster Cove. I don't have anything in common with the people in this town. I've been traveling since Louis died." She was just making it worse. "What did you do in Boston?"

"I was in business, same as Louis."

"Oh. So when you said you went to school with Louis, you didn't mean grade school, you meant Harvard?"

"You look surprised."

"Well, you hardly look like the Harvard type. I mean—"

"You mean the overalls? People on a whaling cruise expect you to dress the part."

So the hayseed farmer was a Harvard grad. Unexpected.

Abby sipped her water and drew a breath. She couldn't look straight on at Tack. It was like staring directly at the sun. He was making her dizzy. But she had to ask.

"So is there a Mrs. Garrity in the picture?"

"Only my mother," Tack answered.

"What about Isabella's mother?" she asked pointedly.

"My mommy went to Heaven, where the angels live," said Isabella as she colored intently on the paper placemats.

"Oh, I'm so sorry. And how old are you, Isabella?"

Isabella put down her crayons and held up five fingers.

Abby nodded. The girl was a treasure. *If she were*

mine, I'd dress her in the cutest clothes. And her tutu wouldn't be on inside out.

Tack observed Abby looking at his daughter.

"She likes to wear the tutu inside out, and she insists on wearing it to school. Her mother was a ballerina."

"I see. How long has she been gone?" Abby whispered to Tack.

"About two years."

So Tack was a widower and had been even longer than she had been a widow.

"How did—" she wondered, then thought better of it in the presence of Isabella.

Tack grimaced. From his uncomfortable look, she surmised there was a story there, but she wasn't going to hear it today.

Abby directed her attention to Isabella. "So, Isabella, what kind of things do you like to do?"

"Sometimes I like to go with my Daddy on the whaling cruise. I like to draw. I'm drawing you now."

Abby leaned in and took a close look at Isabella's picture. She had drawn her dad. There was no mistaking The Incredible Hulk in overalls, a girl with yellow ringlets dressed in a tutu turned inside out, and a stick figure with long strawberry blonde tresses wrapped around her body, like a mermaid, that looked like it could be her.

Isabella studied her. "Are you going to be my new mommy?"

Abby choked on her water. Tack patted her on the back.

"Isabella, don't you think you're getting ahead of yourself? Miss Abigail and I just met."

"But she's very pretty, and I like her. She looks like a mermaid. Is this a date? My daddy doesn't go on many dates. My grandma says he needs to get back into circulation. I can draw a circle. See?"

Abby exploded in laughter.

"I have a feeling I could find out all about you if I asked Isabella the right questions," she said, looking at Tack and biting her bottom lip. She could stare surreptitiously at Tack all day. He was a heartbreaker.

"Nothing to tell."

"Somehow, I doubt that."

The server brought over a basket of lobster fritter appetizers and delivered their lobster roll lunches.

"You're going to love this, Abigail. It's not fancy, but it's delicious."

Tack passed Abby a ramekin of hot melted butter and another with honey lime mustard sauce.

She sliced off a piece of the fried lobster and dipped it into the honey lime mustard sauce. "Mmm. You're right, this is amazing. I need to come into town more often."

Isabella had put her crayons aside and was eating the spaghetti and tomato sauce Katelyn had set in front of her. She was very fastidious. She had on a lobster bib, and she wiped her chin with a napkin each time she took a forkful of spaghetti. The child had manners to spare.

"That's her mom's influence. Her mom used to love to dress Isabella in beautiful clothes. She had big ideas. Now I'm at a loss as to how to fill her shoes."

"Looks to me like you're doing a great job."

Tack seemed pleased to hear it. "So how come I never see you around?"

"I'm hardly ever here. Longley House just doesn't feel like home. I've been drifting. You being a sea captain can probably understand that. I've been restless. I haven't known what to do with myself since Louis died. Now that we've started this gallery, though, it's opened up a whole new world for me."

"Doesn't it get lonely in that big mansion?"

"Well, with four women in the house now, and all that construction going on, it's anything but lonely or quiet. Once the gallery opens, I have a feeling I'll never be alone again."

"Why didn't you build the gallery in town?"

"Well, our gift shop and gallery annex will be in town, at 37 Maple Avenue, but I have acres to spare up at Longley House, so our main gallery will be there. It has such beautiful gardens, and from the upper floors of the house the view of the ocean and Martin Lighthouse is magnificent. I think tourists will want to get a peek inside one of the old mansions. It's not far from here, after all. It's the first house on Hidden Cove Drive."

Tack's eyes twinkled. "I'd like to get a peek inside it myself."

"I'll be sure to send you an invitation to the opening. Are you interested in art?"

"I appreciate beautiful things," he said, staring at her.

Abby looked up from her platter and met Tack's eyes. "What?"

"It's just that I haven't seen anything so lovely in a long time."

Abby smiled broadly at the compliment.

Turning her attention to Isabella, she engaged the child in conversation and found her to be extremely intelligent. The little girl was very talkative and endearing. Her smile lit up the room. Father and daughter were quite the charming duo.

Tack waited for Isabella to finish her sentence before he reentered the conversation. "Since you're opening a gallery, does that mean you're going to stay in Lobster Cove?"

"If you had asked me that a few months ago, I would have said no, because the house was too big and the town was too small. There was nothing for me here. I was thinking of putting it on the market. But now I'm starting to see Lobster Cove through the eyes of my new friends. I guess I'm starting to appreciate it more."

"It's a great town," said Tack. "I couldn't wait to get out of here and go to Boston. That's where I met my wife. She was a dancer in a Boston company. She hated it here, too. There was never enough culture for her. She hated the ocean. She got seasick when I took her out on the boat. We weren't exactly compatible, but she did give me Isabella, and she's the light of my life."

"I can see that."

"My parents are here, and they need me. I've got to save Dad's business, although I'm not sure he even remembers me. But he spent his lifetime building it, and I couldn't stand by and watch it fail…watch him fail. Mom spends most of her time with him, whatever time she can, when she's not watching Isabella."

Abby studied Tack. He was full of surprises.

Katelyn came to the table. "Looks like you kids enjoyed your meal."

Abby and Tack had cleaned their plates. Isabella was still working on her pasta.

"How about some homemade blueberry pie?"

Katelyn suggested.

"It's the best around," Tack said. "Save any room for dessert?"

Abby smiled. "I guess I could handle it."

"We'll have three pieces. Thank you."

"This has been fun," Abby said. "Thank you for lunch." She turned to Isabella. "And I really enjoyed meeting you, Your Highness."

Isabella laughed. "I'm not really a queen," she said, smiling.

"Well, you certainly had me fooled. Tack, I mean it. I had fun. I needed this break."

"I'm glad I ran into you, literally," Tack said. He picked up Abby's hand and held it. "I'd like to—I mean if you want to, I'd like to see you again, Abigail."

Abby's heart opened. She squeezed Tack's hand. "I'd like that, Tack." What was happening to her? She was falling hard and falling fast. For a man she had nothing in common with.

The server brought the dessert plates and forks, and Tack broke contact.

When they had finished their slices of pie, Isabella handed Abby her drawing.

"Here."

"Oh, Isabella, how beautiful! Thank you so much."

"Daddy, are we going out on another date with Miss Abigail?"

Tack's face reddened. "Daddy and Miss Abigail are going to go out on a date together first, and then, we'll see."

Isabella flashed Abigail a smile.

Tack picked up Isabella and faced Abigail.

"Well, would you like to go out on the boat with

me tomorrow? I could use some good luck. Maybe we'll spot a whale."

"Well, I—" Abby was under tremendous pressure to oversee the completion of the gallery, get all the artwork framed, photographed, and hung, plus a million and one other details before the opening. There was so much to do. She couldn't spare a minute, much less a day out on the water. She needed to find someone for the manager position. But there was so much hope on Tack's face. And—God!—it was an amazing face.

She'd been so closed up for so long. Was she ready to take a chance on Tack Garrity? Was this just pure lust? Well, who cared? She had to see Isabella again. The child was amazing. And this was the happiest she'd been since Louis died.

"I'd love to."

Tack glowed, and Isabella clapped.

"The boat leaves Pier 2 at nine a.m. Dress casual."

"I'll see you tomorrow, then."

"It's a date."

Abby watched Tack and Isabella walk down the pier. She couldn't wait until tomorrow to see Tack again.

****

Tack's stomach had just begun to settle when he left the range of Abigail Longley's orbit. How many years had he been waiting to meet this woman in the flesh, and when she finally showed up, what did he do? He rammed into her, like Billy Goat Gruff crossing the bridge, nearly knocking her off her feet. And who did he have in tow but his daughter? Not exactly a recipe for romance. And what was he wearing? Farmer overalls and rubber boots. Smooth, Garrity. That's not exactly how he had envisioned their first meeting. But whether it was serendipity, fate, or mere coincidence, he fully intended to take advantage of this opportunity on their first date tomorrow. She obviously didn't recognize him, and why should she? But *she* was unforgettable.

He removed the faded photograph from the wallet in his overalls, a photograph he'd been carrying around since as long as he could remember. The photograph didn't do her justice. Was it possible she was even more beautiful in person? Her hair was still that brilliant shade of strawberry blonde. It was still long and flowing, with ringlets highlighted by the sun. Not as long as it had been in the picture—she was a college student then—but her face still held that celestial glow, and her body—was there ever a human shape more perfect? Of course, he had imagined her nude most of the time, like the model in the painting, and she had been fully clothed on the dock, but that took nothing away from her appeal. She was a goddess, for sure. She was his Venus, or rather, Louis's Venus. The universe had delivered her as promised, and it was now up to him to make the goddess of love fall in love with him.

Chapter Five

"Do we have any more manager candidates for the Maple Avenue gallery?" Abby asked Victoria over breakfast.

"Oh, I forgot to tell you. Val, the woman you were supposed to interview yesterday, called back right after you left yesterday and said the reason she was a no-show was because she was in an accident."

"An accident? Is she okay?"

"She was pretty banged up. She ran in front of the trolley to save a little boy. The story was all over the *Lobster Cove Anchor*. She'd like to reschedule, if it's okay with you."

"Of course it's all right. Now I feel like an idiot. I spent all day yesterday ranting about the woman. Can you arrange another appointment, if she's willing? I did hang up on her. She probably thinks I'm a first-class bitch."

"Will do, Boss."

"I'm not your boss, Victoria."

"I know, but I like saying it. We are so psyched about being here. Longley House is amazing. The gallery has opened up so many possibilities in our lives. We're indebted to you."

"Well, I'm grateful to all of you. I was just about to close this place up and leave forever. Longley is a hard name to live up to around Lobster Cove. I felt like I was always under a microscope, being scrutinized by Louis's parents and everyone else in the town. And now, losing Louis and his parents in the same year, it's like I'm cursed. Without Louis, I had no desire to live here. There was nothing for me in Lobster Cove."

"The people in town are great," argued Victoria. "You should go down there sometime, meet some of the little people."

Abby laughed. "As a matter of fact, I did go into town yesterday to open up a post office box for us, and I actually ran into one of the 'little' people, as you call them. Only this one was more like a giant."

"Is this giant person responsible for putting that smile on your face and the spring in your step?"

Abby blushed.

"Okay, spill. Tell me everything."

"I can't now. I have to go meet him. We're going whale watching."

"Have you ever been whale watching? You don't strike me as the whale-watching type."

"Well, no, but I'm looking forward to it." Abby grabbed a croissant, took a sip of her orange juice, and bit into a piece of bacon, crispy, just the way she liked it. "I assume Jane is painting today?"

"Yes, and her latest work is fantastic. That cute Ethan Logan is up in the studio with her, *inspiring* her. He's really talented and, according to Jane, not just in the art department."

"Is Jane falling for him?"

"Jane is nuts about him, but she won't admit it, because she doesn't know it yet."

"Keep me posted. How is the construction going?"

"Aidan told Natalie we should be done in a week,

and then she can start moving the furniture in and hanging the paintings."

"That's ahead of schedule," Abby noted. "That Aiden Ames works fast."

"In more ways than one," Victoria admitted. "Those two can't keep their hands off each other."

"Looks like everyone is falling in love again."

"Everyone?"

"Well, I think I may be in *lust* with this sexy sea captain. He literally ran into me yesterday afternoon down at the pier, and we had lunch. He has this darling little girl. I think I'm in love with her. Her name is Isabella. And I can't wait to see her again."

"Will she be there on the cruise?"

"I think she's in school in the mornings and then Tack's mother watches her until he gets back."

"Tack? What a great name for a sailor. What does he look like?"

"He's hard to describe. You'd have to see him to believe him. He's sort of a cross between Paul Bunyan and Hugh Jackman."

"A gorgeous lumberjack? Sounds intriguing."

"That pretty much describes him. Well, got to go. Oh, and what's happening with our new Botticelli?"

"It may not be *our* Botticelli, after all. I didn't want to worry you further until I had confirmation. The lawyer from England is flying in, and he says he has irrefutable proof that the Botticelli you bought from that Berlin art dealer was stolen during World War II. I'm going to listen to what he has to say before I kick him out on his butt. If he wants that painting, he's going to have to pry it out of my hands."

"What's his name?"

"Joshua Waterbury."

"He sounds like a stuffed shirt."

"He's been a real pain in the ass. There's no gray where this guy is concerned. It's black, white, or nothing. According to him, that painting is stolen. It's our *duty* to return it. End of story."

"When is he due to arrive?"

"Later this afternoon. He's booked into that cute little inn, you know, the one they say is haunted—the Sea Crest Inn. It's on a cliff overlooking the cove."

"How long is he going to stay in Lobster Cove?"

"According to him, until he takes possession of the painting."

"Well, call my lawyer, Brandon Fairbanks, with Fairbanks & Fairbanks in Bar Harbor, and have him look into it. See if he's available to consult and sit in on the meeting. In fact, insist on it. I should be back in the early afternoon, so I'll attend that meeting. We can't afford to lose that painting. It's meant to be our biggest draw. We've already advertised it. It's the cornerstone of our collection." Abby laid her napkin by her plate and rose.

"I know. Well, we'll work something out. Have fun."

Abby headed for the door, adding, "And Victoria, I love what you've done with our new Web site and all the publicity you've generated. The virtual tour of the gallery will be a great addition when you get it up, and the interactive features are fantastic. The work you've done with the catalog is really going to boost sales. Your creativity in that area has been monumental."

"I'm so excited about the opening."

"Well, I'm off to spot some whales. Wish me

luck."

"And good luck landing the big fish," Victoria whispered.

Abby walked down to the dock and found Tack's boat, Lobster Cove Adventure Cruises, picking up passengers at Pier 2. Dozens of people were getting ready to board. She saw Tack taking tickets and talking to the passengers. She had to stop and admire him from a safe distance.

"Cripes, he's hot," Abby thought, fanning herself with her hat. She had to get her heart in check before she came face to face with the man. She had already bought a ticket, and she handed it to him as he helped her on board.

"Abby," he said, flashing a wide smile and hugging her. "You didn't have to buy a ticket. You're my guest. Thanks for coming."

"Got to keep Isabella in tiaras," she joked. "Where should I sit for the best view?"

"Up front with me. We're getting ready to head out."

Tack introduced her to his first mate, Andrew, and gave him some final instructions before getting on the loudspeaker system. He announced the itinerary for the day and told the passengers to feel free to enjoy refreshments, look out at the scenery, and watch the film available, narrated by a naturalist, about the whales they'd be seeing.

"And let's hope to God we see some actual whales today," he whispered.

"I'm going to think positive thoughts," Abby said. *But I'd be satisfied just to watch you, Tack.*

"On this first part of the trip we're just heading out

into the ocean to the whale's feeding ground. Hopefully we'll spot some there and won't have to go out too far. I won't have to get back on the loudspeaker until we're closer to our destination. So sit back and enjoy the scenery."

Abby relaxed her tight stomach muscles, applied some sunscreen, donned a sun hat, and sat back to enjoy the view—of Tack. Her heart was jittery, her stomach fluttered, and someone had slapped that goofy grin back on her face. She hoped Tack hadn't noticed. God, the man was built. Today, he'd jettisoned the overalls for a pair of tight-fitting jeans and a body-hugging gray T-shirt, exposing a boatload of rippling muscles. She hoped he didn't want to engage her in conversation, because she doubted she was capable of speech.

"Have a bottle of lemonade," Tack offered. So he'd remembered what she ordered for lunch yesterday. Very considerate.

Abby nodded and pressed the icy bottle against her forehead to cool herself down.

Tack was at the wheel, pointing out interesting sights along the way—lighthouses, lobster fishermen, seals, and seabirds of all kinds, peppered with area history.

"Have you ever been out on a boat along this coast?"

Abby shook her head. "Never had any interest before."

"The coast of Maine is beautiful. It's rugged and isolated. There's so much to see out here. I'm glad I'm the one to show it to you."

Abby relaxed in her comfortable chair. The coast was beautiful. Why had she thought it was desolate and uninteresting? And the seabirds were amazing.

She supposed now was as good a time as any to ask about the former Mrs. Garrity. He was stuck on this boat and couldn't avoid her questions. And she was curious about her competition, dead or not.

"So, do you mind if I ask you some personal questions?"

Tack kept his eyes on the water and shrugged.

"What happened to your wife?"

"She died in a car crash—in Monaco," Tack said.

"Oh, Tack, I'm sorry. Why was she in Monaco?"

"She was dancing in Nice with a French ballet company. That's not the only reason she was in France. She was visiting her former lover. She never got over him, apparently. They were in the car together on a little rendezvous, which just confirmed my suspicions."

Abby was silent.

Tack gripped the wheel and continued. "They broke up when he wouldn't marry her, and she moved to Boston, where we met. When I, um, got her pregnant, I thought I'd do the right thing. But I knew she was still in love with someone else."

"Did you love her?"

"She was beautiful, this dainty creature, as light as a butterfly and apparently as flighty. I was smitten. When Isabella was born, her schedule wouldn't allow her to take care of a baby, so I suggested we move to Lobster Cove. Lobster Cove people are good people, the kind of people I wanted Isabella to grow up with, who exemplify the values I wanted her to learn. But Renata—that was her name—refused to move to Lobster Cove. She didn't want to give up dancing and other men. And I shouldn't have asked her to. But

Isabella needed her mother. Renata was gone all the time. I overheard some of her conversations when she thought I wasn't listening, and I suspected she was meeting her old lover in Nice. I confronted her, and she didn't deny it. She told me she couldn't live in a backwater town like Lobster Cove or she'd turn into a fishwife. She couldn't get over the idea that I would 'waste my time,' as she called it, helping my dad pilot a whaling vessel.

"When she left on that last trip, she told me she was leaving me. I asked her how she could bear to leave Isabella. And it didn't even faze her. We didn't part on good terms, but when I got the phone call that she—they—had been killed in a car crash in France, I still grieved, not so much for myself but because Isabella would grow up without a mother. Still, with Renata gone, there was nothing keeping me in Boston. My dad was in a bad way, and I needed to be there for him and my mother. Dad could no longer take the boat out, so it was up to me. And I've been here ever since."

"Do you ever regret coming back here?"

"Not one day."

"Thanks for telling me, Tack."

"Now, what about you? What did you do after Louis died?"

Abby put down the bottle of lemonade. This was difficult to talk about. And she had never really talked about her feelings with anyone before.

"When Louis died, a part of me died, too," Abby admitted. "I still miss him. He was the most wonderful man. He put up with me, so for that reason alone he was a saint. I was a handful. When he died, I was rudderless. Lobster Cove was not my home, so for the past year I've tried to lose myself, traveling around the world, doing anything to keep from facing the fact that I was alone."

"What about the Longleys?"

"They never thought I was good enough for Louis. After he died, I could tell they wanted me to move out, and I didn't want to be there anyway. Then they were killed in that plane crash. So I had all of Louis's money, and all of theirs, and this big house. I went on a Mediterranean cruise to try to forget, and that's where I met Victoria, Natalie, and Jane, and now we're starting this new exciting venture together. They saved me."

"Did you and Louis ever think about having children?"

Abby took a drink of her lemonade to compose herself.

"All the time. We wanted three, but we tried everything and nothing worked. We couldn't have children."

"You're good with children, good with Isabella. She can't stop talking about you."

"She is very special," Abby said. "When I look at her, I imagine what could have been."

"Would you like to take the wheel?" Tack offered in an abrupt change of subject.

"Me?"

"Why not? We're out on the open water. There's no one around."

Abby took the wheel and felt her spirits lift. She'd never felt so relaxed or so comfortable, not in a long time.

She looked around. "Tack," she screamed. "Over there! Those are whales, aren't they?"

"Hell, they sure are! A pod of great whales and porpoises are following the boat. Here, let me take over."

Tack took the wheel from Abby and made an announcement over the speaker system. "Ladies and gentlemen, we have a pod of great whales on the starboard side. You can see them now, and watch for the porpoises swimming beside the boat." Screams and shouts went up from the passengers.

"Abigail Adams Longley, you're my good-luck charm. You're going to have to come out with me every day."

Abby laughed, crinkled her nose, and bit her lip.

"This is the best day we've had this year. Look at all these whales! This is their feeding area. We'll stay out for another hour and watch them, let the passengers take pictures. Then we'll head back in. This will give them something to talk about back home, enough memories for a lifetime." Pride in his work was evident in Tack's tone. She didn't care if he was poor. He was a good man.

Tack kept the mike and talked about the whales, their habits, and how they related to other wildlife, and Abby squealed and pointed like the rest of the passengers every time one of the monsters surfaced and sprayed.

All the fresh air was making Abby hungry, and Tack seemed to read her mind. He reached into the cooler, brought out a bag, and spread the contents of the lunch he had purchased for Abby on the table. Then he poured her a glass of crisp, cool, sweet white wine.

"This is lovely," Abby said, salivating over the delicate cheeses and fancy crackers, the fruit, and a turkey sandwich on sourdough bread. She ate in silence, enthralled by Tack's knowledge and lulled by his booming voice. She might not know the difference between a humpback whale and a pilot whale, but she was interested in knowing more about the pilot of this particular vessel.

"This is a good sandwich, and the cheese is wonderful. Where did you get all this?"

"From Love Caters All, a sandwich shop and catering business. A friend of mine, Jason Wade, who used to play for the Red Sox, is the prep cook and assistant manager of the food truck they operate in the hospital parking lot. They serve lobster rolls, and they also sell sandwiches. But some of the menu items have a Mexican flair, like *arroz a la tumbada*—similar to paella, *antojitos*—snack foods like *flautas*, *taquitos*, and *tamales*—*quesadillas*, and a special family recipe, a beef stew made with squash and yucca flowers. Mexican can be very romantic. Hard to believe, but people who live in coastal towns can get sick of fish.

"I got the grocery items from the Lobster Cove Grocery Mart and the baked goods from Sweet Bea's," Tack added. "Beatrice O'Brien bakes brown bread, raisin scones, cookies, cakes, and cupcakes. She has a vanilla cake with raspberry filling that's unbelievable. Her meat pies are a favorite with tourists and locals. And you should also try Ned's Lobster Shack. They make great lobster rolls."

"How do you know about all these places and people?"

"Because I live here. I take the time to know all these establishments so I can recommend them to my passengers if they ask, but I also know about them because they're run by my friends. There's some good people in this town, Abigail. You should give it a chance."

"Maybe I will. You really went to a lot of trouble. I appreciate it."

"Thank you."

"So, Tack, what do you do for fun?"

"Sometimes I spend time at the Spinnaker Yacht and Sail Club north of town."

"I've never been there."

"What about the Club?"

"My in-laws belonged to that country club. Louis and I never went there."

"Did you ever attend any events around town?"

"Like what?"

"Like the Harvest of the Sea Festival, or the Lobster Crawl, or the Oil and Water Art Festival?"

"Never heard of any of them."

"The way I feel is if you're going to live in a town, you've got to get to know the people and what's happening in the town. Otherwise, why live there?"

"My feeling is pretty much 'why bother?' "

"I'm going to have to change all that. I'll make it my mission to introduce you to Lobster Cove and Lobster Cove to you."

"Well, you've got your work cut out for you, then."

When they pulled into the pier, the passengers were laughing and thanking the captain and tipping him handsomely. He invited them to come back for the sunset cruise, which he offered several nights a week.

As the last of the tourists rambled along the pier looking for other amusements, Tack helped Abby off the boat. "Abby, this was fun. Thank you for coming with me. When can I see you again?"

Abby stared into his eyes and got lost in them, in that face, as she drank in the sun. Tack tipped back her head and gently kissed her on the lips, and it was electrifying. She felt giddy. She was losing control. She was flying. Or maybe it was the wine.

"Tack," she sighed. Then he deepened the kiss, and her arms flew around his neck as their tongues tangled languorously for several minutes, until—

"Daddy," Isabella cried, running up to him. He scooped her up into his arms and flew her like an airplane around Abigail until she hovered close to Abigail's face. She planted a kiss on Abby's cheek. "Miss Abigail," she said.

"Your Highness."

An attractive elderly woman came up to them. "Aren't you going to introduce me to your *friend*, Tack?"

Tack turned.

"Mother, this is Abigail Longley. Abigail, this is my mother."

Abigail shook Mrs. Garrity's hand. "It's very nice to meet you, Mrs. Garrity."

"Tack's told me nothing about you, but Isabella couldn't stop singing your praises."

Abby's brows rose as she shot Tack an inquisitive glance.

"Don't worry," said Mrs. Garrity. "My son rarely tells me anything. I was sorry to hear about Louis. He was a fine man. And I knew his parents, as well. It's mighty tough, what you've had to endure. It's no wonder you're keeping to yourself."

"Is that what people are saying about me? That I'm

some kind of a recluse?"

"I make it a practice never to take gossip seriously," Mrs. Garrity said. "Everyone grieves in their own way."

"Mom, could you watch Isabella tonight? I have somewhere I have to be."

Mrs. Garrity's eyes sparkled.

"That is, if Abigail will agree to go out with me."

Abby smiled and nodded.

"It's a date," said Isabella excitedly.

"It's been nice to meet you, Abigail."

"You too, Mrs. Garrity."

"Mom, why don't you take Isabella inside? I want to say a proper goodbye to Abigail."

"Don't you have to take the boat back to its berth?"

"I'll have Andrew do that."

Mrs. Garrity took Isabella by the hand, and they walked into the nearby restaurant.

Tack turned to Abigail. "I can't wait to see you again. Will you go out to dinner with me tonight? I have a special spot in mind."

"Yes."

"Then it's a date," he said, echoing Isabella. "Now let's give those gossips something to talk about." With that, he took her in his arms and combed his fingers through her hair, nuzzled her neck, then kissed her lips, making and then breaking contact, teasing her with his tongue, then pulling it away, all the while pressing his body to hers in the most suggestive way. He moved his hands slowly up her sides from her hips, until his fingertips were almost touching her breasts. It was more like foreplay than a see-you-soon kiss, and the encounter left Abigail panting, her nipples straining against her T-shirt, longing for his touch. The warmth of the sunlight and the taste of sweet wine on his lips made her heady with lust. If they hadn't been out in public…

"If only we were alone, Abigail, I would show you—"

He must have read her mind. Left unsaid were the things he would do. She wanted the kiss to go on forever, but Isabella stuck her head out of the restaurant doorway and called, "Come on, Daddy."

He pulled away from her with a regretful smile. "Hold that thought."

How did things move so far so fast? She was no longer in control of her emotions. It was almost as if she were floating in some faraway galaxy. She was falling for Tack at warp speed.

"I'll pick you up at seven this evening," he said, his voice hoarse. "I can't wait."

"Thanks for a lovely day, Tack." She sighed.

"Thank you for the company, Miss Longley. I think my luck is about to change."

Chapter Six

"Mom, how's Dad doing today?" Tack held Isabella's hand while they walked toward his father's room.

"Well, the aide says he's having a good day, although I don't know what's so good about it. He doesn't remember me." He could see the pain in his mother's eyes.

"Mom, don't feel so bad. Half the time he doesn't know who I am, either. But he does remember Isabella. And he always asks me how the whaling is going."

"Thanks for bringing her," Mrs. Garrity said. "I'm glad you could spend some time with your father and relieve me. I've been with him most of the day. He's beginning to tire, but he always perks up for you and Isabella."

"Where else would I be?"

"With that cute new girl of yours?"

"Mom, she's not my girl, not yet, anyway. But I plan to change that soon. Well, Isabella and I are going to say hi to Dad, and then we'll be home. Get some rest. See you later." Tack gave his mother a big hug.

"Bye, Grandma," said Isabella.

"Bye, sweetheart."

Tack watched his mom head toward the front entrance before he and Isabella walked into Ty Garrity's room and sat down on chairs facing his bed.

It broke Tack's heart that this giant of a man had to be confined to this bed in this tiny room, when the great wide ocean had once been his home.

"Hi, Pop," Tack said, taking his father's fragile hand. "Are they treating you right in here? Because if they're not, let me know, and I'll take care of it."

"Who are you?"

Tack's shoulders sagged. His father had gone downhill so rapidly it had happened almost in the blink of an eye. He had fallen on the boat, had to have surgery, and was taken into rehab. Then, in the unfamiliar surroundings, his mind had gone, not gradually but precipitously. First he was forgetful, then he lost his ability to capture words, and then suddenly he had no short-term memory. Sometimes he recognized Tack, and sometimes he didn't. But, miraculously, he always seemed to know Isabella.

"Isabella?" Ty's voice was animated. He looked forward to Isabella's visits. "Come on over and give your old Grandpa a big kiss." Isabella went to her grandfather and wrapped her arms around him.

"And who's that handsome fellow with you? Is that your boyfriend?"

"Grandpa, that's not my boyfriend. That's Daddy."

Ty's face was a mask of confusion.

"Have you graduated college yet?"

"Grandpa, I'm not going to college. I'm only five."

"Of course you are," Ty said. "Well, hold out your hand, Missy. I have a present for you."

Isabella held out her small hand, palm up.

Ty pressed a dollar into it.

"A whole dollar!" Isabella shouted. "Thank you, Grandpa."

"Princess, why don't you go over to that table in the corner and color a picture for Grandpa while we talk," Tack said.

"It's Queen Isabella."

"Sorry, but you'll always be my Princess."

Isabella took her coloring book and crayons and sat down at the table to draw.

Tack pulled his chair closer to his father.

"You're the one who pilots my boat, aren't you?"

"Yes," said Tack. "I'm your son, Tack, remember?"

Tack was met with a blank stare. He didn't care if his dad recognized him. As long as he asked about the boat, Tack was going to keep taking her out.

"Spot any whales today?"

"It was a great day for the whales, Pop. And it was all because of this girl. Her name is Abigail. Abigail Longley." Ty tilted his head as if in recognition. "You remember the Longleys from town, don't you, Pop?"

Ty Garrity closed his eyes.

"Pop, don't fall asleep. I want to tell you about the whales and the girl."

Ty opened his eyes when he heard his son's voice. "Tack!"

"That's right, it's me, Pop." Tack hugged his father. This was huge. His father had recognized him. This period of lucidity would be brief, so he needed to talk fast if he wanted his father to listen to him. He wanted to get his dad's advice.

"We saw dozens of whales. They were surrounding the boat. Yesterday there were none. And the difference was the girl, Abigail. You should see her, Pop. She is, hands down, the most beautiful woman I've ever laid eyes on. Her hair is something else—it's like spun gold, and it just falls around her face like she's a goddess. I'm not kidding, Pop. She has the face of an angel, like that painting in the Uffizi gallery in Florence—*The Birth of Venus*. At first I thought she was a vision, something I had dreamed. But she was real. I touched her. I even kissed her. I'm going to marry her, Pop. Damned if I'm not."

"She's a real looker, like your mother?"

"That's right. Just like that. I'm going to see her again tonight, Pop, because I can't stay away. I only hope I don't go and ruin it by coming on too strong. I hardly know how to act around her. I know we just met, but I feel like she's mine already. I want her to be mine. And you should see how Isabella reacts to her. She's really taken to Isabella. I think she's the one, Pop. I feel it in my heart."

"That's the way it was with me and your mother. I knew she was the one from the second I laid eyes on her. It was like a lightning bolt striking my heart. But you can't get ahead of yourself, son. You've got to let them catch up, wait until they understand how deep your feelings run. Steer the boat slowly. Be gentle. Don't scare her off. Don't scare off the whales."

"That's good advice, Pop." Tack wiped away a tear with the back of his hand.

Ty's eyes glazed over, and he stared straight ahead until they settled on Tack.

"Say, you're the one who pilots my boat, aren't you? Spot any whales today?"

Tack's spirit deflated. "I sure did. I sure did. It was a good day. Isabella, how's that picture coming? Are you ready to come on over and say goodbye to

Grandpa?"

"Sure, Daddy. It's just done." Isabella waltzed over and handed Ty a drawing. "I made a picture for you, Grandpa. It's a picture of you in your boat next to the biggest whale ever. Did you know I'm going to marry the Prince of Whales?"

Ty let out a laugh you could hear down the hall.

"That's my Princess."

Chapter Seven

Abby walked through the new gallery space. "Natalie, this is amazing. You've transformed this place."

"Well, Aidan and his people did all the hard work."

Aidan smiled and gazed at Natalie. "I couldn't have done it without her."

"Aidan, you really outdid yourself," Abby said. "I love these light wood floors, and the natural pond, and the sculpture garden. I can't wait to get the paintings up. The color on the walls is so elegant; it's Palladian Blue, isn't it? It's the perfect shade. And the windows—oh, the light, both natural and artificial. The effect of the glass and stone, the marble and wood surfaces with the track lighting—it just sparkles. It's everything I envisioned. The beautiful arches throughout the space were an inspired touch. And you've managed to remain true to the original standards of Longley House."

"My grandfather built Longley House," Aidan reminded her. "She's an historic treasure."

Before adding the gallery, Abby had always thought of the house as a mausoleum, a lonely old fossil that would be better shuttered. Now, people in town could visit the gallery at the mansion and enjoy the beauty of art from around the world.

"Let my crew clear away their tools and vacuum up

the sawdust, and then we can complete painting the wainscoting and the rest of the wall panels in the next room. After that, we start hanging the paintings, covering the floors with the oriental carpets, and placing the antique furniture and Chinese porcelain vases. I like your idea of placing couches and chairs in each room so people can relax while they're looking at the paintings."

Aidan led Abby and Natalie toward the back entrance of the gallery. "Let me show you the limestone floors leading out into the garden. I placed some concrete benches by the water so patrons could enjoy a view of Martin Lighthouse with some ocean beyond."

Abby clapped. "This is fabulous! I can't wait until the opening. I've gone over the menu with Chef, and we'll decide on a caterer in the next day or two. Victoria is ready to send out the invitations, and we've received the stock for the gift shop. Aidan, how is the Maple Avenue storefront coming?"

"Why don't you come on down and check it out for yourself," he offered. "It's sort of a mini version of the gallery here. Light wood floors, same paint colors. A nice selection of paintings, representing only a fraction of what we offer here at Longley House. It will give visitors a bird's-eye view of the main gallery. What we have on Maple Avenue is really a microcosm of the artwork here at Longley House. And with the addition of the Longley collection, we almost have a mini-museum. It's an exciting concept."

"I can't believe the progress you've made here. I will be down to see the Maple Avenue shop later this afternoon. Aidan, you have my eternal gratitude."

Aidan looked adoringly at Natalie. "Natalie was

my inspiration."

Oh, brother! The hormones in the room are as thick as the layers of sawdust. "Have you seen Victoria?"

Natalie wrinkled her nose. "Yes, she's waiting for you in the study with that pompous Englishman, Joshua Waterbury."

"Where's our prize painting?"

"On an easel, covered with a drop cloth, just like you asked."

"I can't say I'm looking forward to this encounter. The man sounds like a rude boor." Abby grimaced.

"Good luck, Abby," Aidan said before he took Natalie's hand and led her through the gallery and out the back entrance.

Steeling herself, Abby strode down the hall to the study. She and her new partners had scoured the continent, shopped estate sales, attended art auctions, trudged all over Europe to meet the artists themselves wherever they painted—Paris, Prague, Provence. Perhaps the easiest purchase had been through that eccentric Berlin art dealer, and now there was an authentication issue with it, her favorite painting. Just her luck.

If they lost that painting, she'd have no choice but to raid the private Longley collection. She was a Longley by marriage, but those paintings had been in Louis's family for decades, and she didn't feel right offering them for sale. She was planning to display the Longley collection, much of it priceless European master works, in the tradition of the Isabella Stewart Gardner Museum, the art museum and gallery in Boston. Abby felt the weight of her briefcase with the papers she'd brought from Berlin. The prize painting was absolutely essential to the gallery. She was prepared to do battle.

When she stepped into the study, Victoria and Joshua sat on either side of the room, each with arms crossed, glaring at one another. How long they had been in that pose was anyone's guess. Their body language spoke volumes. They were locked in adversarial hell.

"Abby," Victoria breathed and loosened her arms. "I'd like you to meet Joshua Waterbury. Mr. Waterbury is here about the Botticelli."

Abby deposited her briefcase on the conference table with a thud. She shook Joshua Waterbury's hand, assessing him doubtfully. "Mr. Waterbury."

"Mrs. Longley," he responded in an equally noncommittal tone.

Joshua Waterbury was younger than she'd expected, good looking, with tufts of dark curly hair, spectacles, and broad shoulders. Unfortunately, he looked likeable, and her first impression was that he was honest, damn him. She really wanted to hate the man.

"Let's get right to the point, ladies. Unfortunately, the painting you have purchased and currently have in your possession—Sandro Botticelli, *Portrait of Venus*, oil on canvas, Florence—is stolen. The portrait was coerced from a Jewish family by a Nazi officer in Vienna during World War II. The officer displaced the family, had them transported to a concentration camp, while he and his family took over not only the house but all its possessions, including the painting in question."

Abby was horrified. "How could that have happened? I assume you have proof of this?"

"Irrefutable proof, I'm afraid," stated Waterbury. "It's all outlined in these documents." He handed Abby the papers. "And these are just documents. Behind each of those pieces of paper is a personal story, a story of loss, countless tragedies, and great injustices I could spend a lifetime correcting. Do you know that an estimated 650,000 works of art were plundered, looted by the Nazis from the Jews?"

Abby was flabbergasted. On the surface, Mr. Waterbury appeared to be sincere. Abby reviewed the papers and frowned.

"I legitimately bought this painting from Franz Heidegger of Berlin not two months ago. Here is the bill of sale and proof of provenance." Abby handed over her documents for Mr. Waterbury's inspection.

Mr. Waterbury read the correspondence and cleared his throat. "Mrs. Longley, these documents appear to be in order. But as I told Mrs. Dare, Herr Heidegger has been detained for questioning in Berlin. We have found dozens of works of art in the basement of his apartment, priceless paintings by Old Masters, Renaissance painters, Impressionists. These paintings are all of questionable provenance. We are trying to establish how he acquired such gems in the first place, probably for next to nothing. We're convinced it was through nefarious means. The heirs, the innocent victims, need to be compensated. "

"I was under the impression that Herr Heidegger's father had been a legitimate dealer," Abby challenged.

"If you consider working for Hitler legitimate," Mr. Waterbury commented with a hint of sarcasm.

"Unfortunately, some people try to rewrite history."

"My father-in-law, Jonathan Longley, dealt with him quite often to add to his private collection. When we were in Berlin earlier this summer, we dropped into the son's apartment, and he offered me a selection of paintings."

"Mrs. Longley, may I see the painting now?"

Abby walked over to the easel and removed the drop cloth. When it fell away, Mr. Waterbury gasped, obviously overcome with emotion. He studied the painting and the signature.

"It's the missing Botticelli."

"Missing?" Abby inquired. "What do you mean?"

"Let me explain," Mr. Waterbury began. "In Botticelli's early pagan phase, he fell in love a young Italian Renaissance noblewoman named Simonetta Vespucci, reputed to be the most beautiful woman in Florence in her day. She was known as 'la bella Simonetta.' And as you probably know, she was the model for some of his most famous paintings, including *The Birth of Venus*." Joshua stared at Abby and coughed.

"Did anyone ever tell you that you bear a strong resemblance to Simonetta? In fact, you, er, look so much like Simonetta, it's uncanny. Botticelli painted dozens of pictures of her, most in the nude or as he imagined her in the nude. They were for his eyes only. Whether or not they were lovers has not been substantiated. She died at age twenty-three, and he requested to be buried at her feet. This painting was presumed burned in the Bonfire of the Vanities in 1497 in Florence, when fundamentalist Girolamo Savonarola, an Italian friar and preacher, urged the artists of his day to burn their lascivious images. We will always wonder what the art world missed when Botticelli burned some of his early paintings. But apparently someone from the church who was a friend of the Medici family must have rescued it, hidden it, preserved it. One of the Medici brothers was also in love with Simonetta. And all these years we thought this image had been destroyed. But it was obviously in someone's private collection and passed down through the centuries.

"The portrait was stolen by the Nazis during World War II, confiscated by the Nazi general while he was assigned to Vienna," Mr. Waterbury explained. "Eventually Herr Heidegger's father, one of Hitler's favored art dealers, was able to buy it at a reduced price, and he has hoarded it ever since. But recently, a claim was filed for this painting by a survivor of the camps. A member of a family we thought had gone up in ashes at Auschwitz."

"A survivor has come forward to claim the painting?" Abby asked incredulously.

"Yes. The youngest son of a prominent banking family somehow managed to survive the camps, and when he returned to Vienna, someone else was living in his house. Everything of value, including the paintings, had been removed. *Portrait of Venus* was on a bill of sale from the Nazi officer to Herr Heidegger's father, who needed money when he fled the Russians at the end of the war. Only after the claim was filed did we learn of the painting's existence. But there's no record of any 'sale' by this banking family to the Nazi officer. Obviously it was confiscated or taken under duress, as many works of art were at the time. Even if Herr Heidegger indeed has proof of his father's purchase, the painting was not the officer's to sell."

Abby looked at Victoria in resignation. If these documents were legitimate, then this painting should be in the hands of its rightful owner, the sole survivor of the family almost completely destroyed in the Holocaust.

"The survivor remembers the painting in his house as he was growing up. It was his mother's favorite. He is elderly now, in need of money for medical expenses. He is willing to sell the painting. There is something else. The Uffizi Gallery in Florence has expressed an interest in adding this piece to their collection to place in Hall 10/14 with *The Birth of Venus* and *Primavera,* Botticelli's other paintings."

Abby recalled their recent visit to the Uffizi. Yes, that's where the painting belonged. It was perfect for the Venus Gallery, it was beautiful, but it wasn't theirs to keep. This development changed everything.

"I can understand your dilemma, Mrs. Longley. You purchased this painting in good faith. You paid more than a million dollars for it. This painting is priceless. If we could put a value on it, it would be millions of euros. Imagine, a missing Botticelli, found after all these centuries. And the Uffizi Gallery is willing to pay you. You'd make a handsome profit."

"But the opening…" Abby said.

"And, of course, you may borrow it for the opening."

Abby rubbed her forehead. "You'll understand if I want my attorney to review these papers for authenticity."

"Of course."

"He should be arriving any minute."

Abby examined the tempera on canvas. It was mesmerizing, a miniature of the model used in *The Birth of Venus*. It was a masterpiece. And looking at the painting was like looking in a mirror.

There was a knock on the study door.

"Abigail?" Abby's attorney, Brandon Fairbanks, entered, and Abby made the introductions. Before he settled at the table, the attorney went to the painting, drawn to it as anyone would be, to the beauty of the model and to the rich colors, still vibrant after so many centuries.

"Abby, this model looks exactly like you. The resemblance is amazing."

"That's what people keep telling me."

Once seated, Brandon studied the papers Abby handed him and huddled head to head with Joshua Waterbury.

Abby tapped her feet. Agitated, she wondered whether having a borrowed painting would affect her gallery opening. Not if Mr. Waterbury kept his word.

Brandon interrupted her thoughts. "I'm sure you are aware, Mr. Waterbury, that there is a thirty-year statute of limitations on making claims on stolen property."

"Of course, but we could hold you up in court indefinitely," Waterbury replied. "And time is running out for the heir I represent. He might not live to see his family vindicated. That would be a tragedy he shouldn't have to suffer twice."

Brandon gave him an assessing look before advising, "That being said, Abby, the papers appear to be legitimate. If you are agreeable, would you like me to execute the sale to the Uffizi and have them compensate the survivor?"

"It's the right thing to do, I know that. I want to do what's fair, and I know this is right, but—" Abby took a last wistful glance at the portrait and nodded.

"I will get the documents ready for your signature," said Brandon. "Meanwhile, you may keep the painting until after the opening. Mr. Waterbury will stay until then, and he will personally hand-deliver our looted art to the rightful owner and then on to the Uffizi."

Abby nodded.

"Victoria, thank you," Mr. Waterbury said. "Please, allow me to take you and Mrs. Longley to dinner tonight. I'm new in town, and I'd love the company."

"I already have plans," Abby said. "Vickie, why don't you join Mr. Waterbury for dinner, and you can discuss plans to hand over the painting."

Victoria nodded, unsmiling.

"I must to be going." Abby sighed, staring longingly at the priceless painting that now belonged to history. She wiped away a tear.

Mr. Waterbury looked relieved. It was obvious he didn't like being at odds with Victoria. He had been sneaking looks at her throughout the negotiations, showing telltale signs of attraction—loosening his tie, combing his fingers through his hair, adjusting his glasses, perspiring profusely, staring longingly. Well, why not? Victoria was a stunning woman.

Abby glanced at her watch. Tack would be picking her up soon. She needed to get dressed for dinner and get out of her casual "whaling" clothes. She'd run out of time to visit the Maple Avenue storefront and see the progress Aidan had made. She'd have to do that tomorrow. She also needed to check in with Jane. She hadn't seen Jane all day. Jane was holed up in her loft, painting her heart out and probably cozying up to Ethan Logan. Well, she could certainly spare a few minutes. And she wanted to see how Jane was getting on.

Abby knocked on Jane's studio/bedroom door. She heard rustling sounds, shoes scuffling, paint brushes rattling. What was going on in there? Was she interrupting a tryst? Jane and Ethan had deadlines they had to meet for the opening. There was no time to fool around. She knocked again, this time with more force.

Jane came to the door, her hair mussed, specks of paint on her nose.

"Abby." The sound whooshed out of Jane's mouth.

"Is everything all right in here?" Abby craned her neck to peek around the door. The easel was covered. Then she noticed a large man's tennis shoe halfway under the bed. "I hope you two are working on your paintings. The opening is only a few weeks away. Before then, these paintings have to dry and be framed."

"We'll be ready," said Jane, who was immovable.

"May I come in?"

"Well, um, actually—"

"What are you hiding in there?"

"It's a surprise."

"Somehow, I'm not surprised. I'll come back tomorrow."

"Okay, well, bye, then." Jane shut the door in Abby's face. Well, artists were temperamental, a breed unto themselves. They could be expected to be strange. But Jane was hiding something, and Abby was determined to find out what it was.

Chapter Eight

She hadn't been on a date, a real date—not a whaling trip with hundreds of people tagging along, but a real private date—since Louis had died. She didn't feel like she was betraying Louis. Louis would want her to be happy. He was a generous man. And she had been miserable for the past twelve months. Long enough.

Since she'd run into Tack, she'd been experiencing some strange emotions. She enjoyed being around him. She was attracted to him. That kiss on the docks had awakened her senses. She felt it deep down in her soul. If he had continued his seduction a minute longer, she would have submitted to him right there on the pier, gossipers or no gossipers. She was afraid the attraction to Tack might be partially because she adored Isabella. But she had to admit she couldn't wait to see Tack again.

She had no idea where he was taking her. Another fried-fish shack? There were probably dozens of those around town. He hadn't even given her a clue. Should she dress up? Would he be dressed in overalls? She didn't care. In fact, she was anxious to see what he looked like without the overalls—better yet, sans any clothes. If she dressed up, would he think she was stuffy? His first impression of her was that she was a snooty, stuck-up bitch who thought she was too good for Lobster Cove. Well, she was who she was, and

Abigail Adams Longley wouldn't be caught dead without her fancy clothes and jewelry, so let him get a taste of the *real* Abigail. Hmm, that sounded naughty. Tack was the ultimate Marlborough Man. Rugged, handsome, and simple. No doubt he had been a Boy Scout. Abigail Adams Longley was complicated. So if he intended to continue seeing her, he'd better get used to it, because she was about to complicate his life.

Tack arrived right on schedule. She liked a punctual man. And he was carrying flowers and wearing a well-tailored suit.

She accepted the flowers and put them in a vase.

"Wow," said Tack. "You look amazing in that dress, and those shoes." She was glad she'd elected to dress up and wear the high heels. Tack was tall enough.

"And you look good, too." Why be coy? He looked good enough to eat. And she was hungry.

"You mean without the overalls?"

"That's not what I meant. Do we have time for a tour?"

"Sure. I'd like to see where the other half lives."

"Well, we're still under construction in the gallery, but it's really shaping up. I'll show you that another time, but let's see the rest of the house."

"More like a mansion. Lead the way," said Tack, grabbing her hand.

Abby didn't like to be manhandled, but for some reason she didn't mind this close encounter with Tack.

"I'd introduce you to my friends, but they all seem to be out tonight. Longley House has turned into a sorority sleepover. All hormones, all the time."

"Is that a problem for you?"

"On the contrary. I hated it until they got here. It

was becoming unbearable. I was half ready to sell it and move somewhere, anywhere. But now it seems like home. I guess it's the company and the gallery. It's breathed new life into all of us. I think Louis would have been proud of me, that I'm moving on with my life." Moving on in more ways than one, she thought. Tonight, with Tack, would be a turning point. Abby wiped a tear from her cheek.

After they toured the kitchen, living room, dining room, study, and the rest of the rooms on the lower floor, they took the elevator to the second floor, where Abby showed Tack the guest bedrooms where her friends were staying, all of them except Jane, who occupied the tower bedroom on the ocean side of the house, which doubled as her artist-in-residence studio.

"What about your bedroom?" Tack asked pointedly, as if he were ready to get an early start on the evening.

"I couldn't stay in the bedroom where I lived with Louis. Not anymore. So I had Aidan redesign my space on the third floor." She led him into the spacious area.

"Your closet is bigger than my bedroom," Tack said, as he walked over to the window. "And this view is amazing. You can see the ocean in every direction."

Abby was glad Tack approved. If things went well at dinner, she planned to invite him back here. That made her curious about where he lived.

"You can come back during the day to see the garden. Maybe by then we'll have the gallery finished. You can bring Isabella and your mom to the opening, if you want."

"They wouldn't miss it. I know they'd love it. Well, we'd better get going. We have reservations at a restaurant outside of town. I hope you haven't been to the Crow's Nest."

Abby turned off the lights and led the way back downstairs.

"I haven't been to any restaurants around here, except for Mariner's Fish Fry with you."

"Not in all these years?"

"I told you, Chef prepares all the meals."

"If you want to go to a restaurant, you probably take the family plane and jet off to France."

Abby blushed.

"I was just kidding," Tack said. "You mean you've done that?"

"Louis loved to surprise me."

Tack's shoulders sagged. "Well, then I hope this dinner isn't anticlimactic. A friend of mine from Boston just opened the place. I helped him find the property. It has a great view of the water, but I guess nothing would come close to the view from Longley House."

"Tack, it sounds lovely. I am looking forward to it, and to spending time with you." She might as well have said, *Okay, take me now.*

Abby locked up the house and unlocked her heart. She was taking a chance on Tack, but it was a chance she wanted to take.

"I'll bet you have some garage. I heard the Longleys collected cars."

"It's a ten-car garage, and yes, there are cars of all makes and models down there. I rarely take one out."

"I'm afraid you'll have to settle for my BMW." Tack helped Abby into the passenger seat.

"It's a wonderful car," Abby said and meant it. She wondered how Tack could afford this nice a car on what he made as a boat captain. Exorbitant car payments, no doubt.

Tack pulled out onto Hidden Cove Drive in front of the Longley House and drove about five miles out of town.

"Isn't this a little off the beaten path?" Abby asked, as the car climbed higher. "It's almost in Acadia National Park."

"Yes, it's at the edge of the park and on a cliff overlooking the ocean, and that's the beauty of it—it's remote and romantic."

Abby swallowed. Romantic. Hmmm. Interesting.

When they arrived, Tack turned his car over to the valet and came around to help Abby out.

"And did I tell you that you look amazing tonight?"

"Yes, you did. But a girl can't have enough compliments." Her black sheath showed off her trim legs and bare shoulders, but it was cool up in the mountains, so she was glad she'd brought along a wrap.

When they walked into the restaurant, they were greeted by a man about the same age as Tack—and Louis, had he lived.

He hugged Tack and offered his hand to Abby.

"Who is your date, and how much did you have to pay her to go out with you, Garrity?"

"Cut it out, Reardon. Abigail Longley, this is Caleb Reardon, the *friend* I was telling you about. He owns the restaurant."

Caleb's brows rose, and he looked at Tack, who shook his head.

"It's a pleasure to meet you, Abigail. Any relation to *the* Longleys of Lobster Cove?"

"Abby was married to Louis Longley," Tack said,

turning to Abby. "She lives at Longley House in town. Abby, Caleb also went to school with Louis."

"And by school, I assume you mean Harvard."

"That's right," Caleb replied. "I did some deals with Louis. I was sorry to hear he had died. And then his parents. Double whammy. You have my sincere condolences."

"Thank you, Caleb."

"I've reserved our best table for you two tonight." He led them to a cozy table at the back of the restaurant, where a large picture window gave a scenic view of Acadia National Park.

Tack seated Abby, and she admired the vista. "This is lovely. I had no idea this was up here."

"Well, we just opened, but we have people coming all the way from Bar Harbor." Judging by the number of diners who were already seated, it looked like the new venture was going to be very successful.

"Let me bring over a bottle of our best champagne—on the house, of course. Are you celebrating anything special?"

Abby looked up at Tack.

Tack held her hand across the table. "Any night with Abigail is special."

"Smooth, Tack," Caleb quipped. "And where did you rent the suit? I'm glad you're respecting our no-overalls policy."

"I happen to own this suit," Tack countered.

"Glad to hear it. I'll send over the waiter to take your order."

"Tack, this place is lovely. The view of Acadia National Park and the ocean at sunset is breathtaking. And the sparkling lights on the patio—what a lovely touch. Live music…and the décor is stunning. Your friend has done everything right."

"Let's drink to that. You know, Abigail, there's a lot to like about Lobster Cove."

And there's a lot to like about you. "What was that secret message passing between you two a minute ago?"

"Nothing," Tack said dismissively.

What are you hiding, Tack Garrity?

"The artwork on the walls is wonderful. Someone has very good taste."

"I'll pass on your compliments to Caleb."

"So you two met at Harvard Business School?"

"Yes. Caleb not only owns the business but is a celebrity chef. He owns several restaurants around the country."

"I don't know much about cooking, so I'm not familiar with him. I imagine Chef would be."

"I'm sure."

"So, how's Isabella?" Abby asked.

"I think you're more interested in my daughter than in me."

"That's not true. But there's just something about her. I can't get her out of my mind."

The sommelier arrived, uncorked a bottle, and poured the sparkly liquid into two crystal champagne flutes before them. "Mr. Garrity?"

"It's wonderful, Jacques, thank you."

"You're on a first-name basis with the sommelier?"

The server came over with two menus. "Mr. Garrity? Would you like to hear the specials tonight?"

"Of course, Brady."

"And the server?"

"I've been here before."

She wondered with whom. Had he been here with a date?

"Abby, I could recommend the duck or the trout. I've had both."

Abby studied the menu.

"I think I'll start with the lobster bisque. We are in Lobster Cove, after all. And I love duck, so I'll try that. Thank you."

"And I'll have a Caesar salad and the trout," said Tack. "We'll have an order of the *haricot vert* with herb butter also, please. And bring out some of those delicious popovers."

"Sure thing, Mr. Garrity."

The fact that he pronounced green beans in perfect French didn't escape her. There was more to Tack Garrity than met the eye. But she wondered what it would take to shake out his secrets. And she was convinced there were some. A pilot of a whaling boat who wears overalls and rubber boots by day and transforms into a debonair, French-speaking man of the world, who drives a BMW sports car, by night? Something was wrong with this picture.

Abby sipped her champagne. "This is divine, Tack. Everything about this place, is so—unexpected. And so is everything about you. So what are you hiding? Are you a wanted fugitive—a bank robber—hiding out in an obscure backwater town?"

"I'm an open book, Abby. And I wouldn't exactly call Lobster Cove a backwater town. After all, your in-laws were one of the richest couples on earth, and they chose to live here."

"Their ancestors came over on the Mayflower,

literally. They only tolerated me. I think they thought of me as a changeling even though I am a descendant of John Adams and named after Abigail Adams, the second First Lady of the United States. They were in a perpetual state of prune-faced disappointment because I couldn't give Louis children—heirs—and they blamed me, although it was never determined definitively whose fault it was. I know they hoped Louis would tire of me. But that was never going to happen. Louis never would have left me, unless he had no choice, which in the end, was exactly what happened."

"I doubt that. You are a beautiful, sophisticated woman. I'm sure they loved you. Still, I don't think you're giving this town a chance. It's no Paris, but I don't think I'd want to live anywhere else on earth or raise my child anywhere else."

"Really? Not even if you had all the money in the world?"

Tack pursed his lips.

Now she'd insulted the man. *Abby, will you ever learn not to lord it over people less fortunate?* It was obvious he could barely make ends meet. He was working on a boat to salvage his father's business. He looked amazing, and his suit fit like a glove, but he'd probably rented it and those beautiful Italian leather shoes. *He'll probably have to take them back before midnight or he'll turn into a pumpkin. Most likely, he'll have to earn a month's salary to pay for this dinner.* He couldn't even afford regular clothes for his daughter. She had to wear a tutu to school, inside out. Dammit. His friend had to treat them to the champagne to make it look like he could afford to be here in this high-toned place, while she had all the money in the world.

Dropping some of it on a dinner at a place like this wouldn't mean anything to her, but to Tack it would be everything. Poor Tack. He wanted to impress her. He was so sweet. But it was heartbreaking. She'd pick up the check but that would be even more embarrassing to him. Still, she was falling hard for the man. In fact, she wanted to take him into her arms right now.

The waiter brought her lobster bisque and Tack's Caesar salad.

She tasted the soup. "This is wonderful, better than any I've ever tasted. I'm serious."

"I told you, Caleb is a first-class chef."

"How's your salad?"

"Delicious. Crisp. Excellent."

The two ate in silence until the next course arrived. She was calculating what this meal was going to cost him. She should have ordered something less expensive than the duck.

Her first mouthful of duck delighted her taste buds. "This duck is perfectly cooked and flavored. It's so fresh."

"Again, I'll tell Caleb you're pleased. So tell me more about how this gallery enterprise came about."

"Well, I was on a Mediterranean cruise. We were in Florence at the Uffizi Gallery, and the four of us were all standing there gawking over *The Birth of Venus*. That's one of the famous Botticelli paintings hanging at the gallery in Florence."

"I'm familiar with Sandro Botticelli," Tack said in a deadpan voice.

Shit. He thinks I think he's a hayseed. I've got to stop being so condescending, just because I'm worldlier than he is. This date is not going the way I thought it would. Maybe it will never work out. We're so different. But she felt something when she was with Tack and Isabella. Isabella. What she wouldn't give to have a child as sweet as Isabella.

"Well, that particular painting meant something special to each of us," Abby said. "We had been on several excursions together, yet not *together*. We were each alone on the cruise, but we found we had the same taste in art—in everything, as it turned out. I invited them out for coffee after our visit to the Uffizi, and we discovered we were all widows. Another thing we had in common. We were all at loose ends. We're all interested in art, and Jane is a gifted artist. Suddenly it just clicked. I had this idea about the gallery. I had this big house, and wads of money, and nothing to do with it. It was a revelation. It just made perfect sense."

Shit. There she went again. She had wads of money, and he was fighting to keep his head afloat. How insensitive could she be?

She swallowed and tried to dislodge the lump of guilt bouncing in the pit of her stomach and wallowing at the bottom of her throat.

"We've spent the past three months traveling, acquiring art, meeting with the architect, building out the gallery, and having a great time. The other women are lovely. I can't wait for you to meet them."

"And I assume you are footing the bill for this entire enterprise? Is this all a game to you? You're toying with people's lives. What if you suddenly tire of your little project? Where does that leave these other women? Homeless, out of a job?"

Abby was shocked. "Where is all that anger coming from? You don't know me if you think this is a game. I'm totally invested in this project, and I don't mean monetarily but emotionally. I think I'd like to go home now." How disappointing to find the chink in Tack Garrity's armor so soon. Well, better late than never.

"I'm sorry," he apologized. "I stuck my foot in my big mouth again."

Abby was adamant. "I think we're done here. Please take me home."

"Abigail, please give me another chance." Tack grabbed her arm across the table. "I am truly sorry. I didn't mean it like that. I don't know why I said that. Please, stay. We haven't even had dessert."

Abby's eyes narrowed. Was dessert a euphemism for sex? Because if it was, then he was way off base. She was attracted to him. More than attracted, but Louis had never gotten angry with her. And here they were fighting on their first date. She didn't need this aggravation. She crossed her arms and pouted for a minute.

"Now you remind me of my ex-wife," Tack said. "She was a world-class pouter."

Abby's mouth opened in surprise. "Well, we all know how much you thought of your ex-wife. I would never have cheated on you. Don't put me in the same category."

"It's just that you are—well, fancy, like her."

"Go ahead, say it, Tack," Abby interjected. "Fancy is just another word for snobby and stuck-up and self-centered and privileged. So why the hell do you even want to go out with me?"

Some of the other restaurant patrons were turning to look at them.

"Because," said Tack, lowering his voice and rubbing her arm in a circular motion. "You're the most beautiful woman I've ever met."

"Your wife was beautiful."

"How do you even know that?"

"I looked her up on the Internet. She was an accomplished ballerina."

Tack smiled. "You looked me up on the Internet? I'm flattered."

"Don't be. I definitely did not look *you* up on the Internet. I looked up your wife. And don't you dare patronize me. I asked you a simple question. Why bother with me?"

"Because," Tack continued, "you're fiery and you're smart and you're driven, and I can't wait to kiss you again. In fact, I'd miss dessert for another sample of what we had on the pier this afternoon."

Abby blew out a breath. "So, you're horny, and I'm available."

"That's not what I said or meant. You're driving me crazy, Abigail Longley."

The waiter crept up to the table.

"Would anyone care for dessert or coffee, on the house, courtesy of the chef?"

Abby shook her head. The man couldn't even afford dessert. Okay, she was going to order dessert, the most expensive selection on the menu, and coffee, and maybe an after-dinner drink—because she was never going to see Tack Garrity again.

The waiter handed them dessert menus.

"Anything look interesting?"

"Yes, I'll have the house special. Surprise me," Abby said.

"I'll have the same."

Abby tried to make herself smaller at the table. She shut her lips tight as a clam and stared daggers at Tack. She huffed and hissed, "You do not know how to treat a lady, which is why you will never get another date with me and is probably why you can't get a date with any other woman, which is why you're so horny."

Tack started laughing.

"For your information I could have any woman I want. But I don't want *any* woman. I want you, dammit."

"You are priceless, Tack Garrity. And conceited. The only females sniffing around you are whales. And you can't even manage to spot any of those."

At that point the waiter came to the table with a scrumptious-looking confection that consisted of gelato, chocolate, and fruit in an edible almond basket, under a mound of whipped cream.

Abby looked at Tack. He said she was driving him crazy. Well, let's see what he thinks of this. She swiped a dollop of the whipped cream with her forefinger and slowly touched it to her tongue, letting it linger there. Then she licked the whipped cream off her fingers.

Tack was mesmerized.

"I hope you get an eyeful, Tack Garrity, because this is the closest you're going to get to my tongue, tonight or ever." She licked her lips and proceeded to taunt him.

She repeated her suggestive display, this time with a strawberry dipped in chocolate.

"Christ, Abby. You're a difficult woman."

"Take that back."

"I will not."

"I am not difficult!"

Furious, Abby threw a spoon at Tack across the table, and it landed with a thud against his chest, splattering melted chocolate and strawberry juice all over his white shirt. "Ha," she spat.

"Abigail Longley, you deserve to be spanked like a naughty child."

"Don't you dare lay a hand on me, Tack Garrity. You're nothing but a big brute. I am a civilized woman, but you make me so mad I want to spit and throw things."

"You are a bit of a banshee," Tack said, trying not to smile.

"I think we're done here. Obviously we rub each other the wrong way."

Tack took her hand and rubbed his thumb across her palm. "That is not the way I want to rub you."

Abby pulled her hand out of Tack's grasp as though she'd been scalded. He was trying to stir her up—and it was working.

"That is crass, even for you, Tack Garrity."

Suddenly the waiter appeared with the check, and Tack slapped down his credit card.

"Tell the chef the dinner was excellent."

"Yes, Mr. Garrity."

Abby marched out of the restaurant, amid stares, and tapped her foot impatiently on the pavement at the valet stand. Tack chased after her, breathing hard, and handed the valet his ticket. "It's the blue BMW, please."

"Yes, Mr. Garrity."

"Does everybody in this restaurant know you?"

Tack fumed. "Why do you care?"

"I don't. Now take me home, straight home. No detours to your house, which I'm sure is nothing but a man cave, a web where you trap unsuspecting women in your lair."

"What did you say? Do you know how juvenile you sound?"

"I know exactly what kind of man you are."

"You don't know anything about me," Tack countered.

Well, she wasn't going to see his house tonight, and he wasn't going to be invited back to her bedroom. She didn't want to see where he lived. She was sure it was a hovel, and she pictured that poor darling Isabel having to endure living with a father who had the temperament of an angry bear awakened before he'd completed his hibernation.

She reached for the handle of the car door, but the valet stepped up.

"Allow me."

"Thank you," Abby huffed. "At least one of you is a gentleman."

Tightening her seatbelt, she sat there with her arms folded and mouth welded tight. Tack started the car, gunned the engine, and drove down the highway, exceeding the speed limit.

"Well, aren't you going to say anything?" Tack asked.

"What do you want me to say?"

"How about, for starters, I had a wonderful dinner, the food was great, and I'm sorry I threw a spoon at you, ruining your best white shirt."

Abigail exclaimed, "I'm not sorry about any of it. I will admit the dinner was good *in spite* of you."

Tack barreled down the road in silence until he pulled up in front of Longley House, slammed on the brakes, and shut off the engine.

"You are a spoiled brat, Abigail Longley. I don't know why I even bother with you. This is not the way I wanted this night to end."

As Abby unhooked her seatbelt and tried to open the passenger car door, Tack pressed the auto lock, then reached over and grabbed her shoulders. She was trapped.

"We are not done here."

"I think we are," yelled Abby. "And now I know why your wife cheated on you. You're an overbearing control freak."

"My wife left me because she died. At least get your story straight."

"You look like you want to slap me, Tack," Abby taunted. "Why don't you just go ahead and do it?"

"Because as soon as you stop talking I'm going to tell you exactly what I want to do to you."

Abby opened her mouth to a perfectly formed O. In one motion, Tack slid back the driver's seat, pulled her roughly across the console and positioned her astride his lap. His breathing was ragged.

Her heart was beating like a drum, and she could feel his erection pulsing as he positioned her on top of it. She squirmed as he started to grind against her.

He pushed up her dress, pulled down her panties, and kissed her while he stroked her until she was wet. She threw her arms around his neck, kissed him back greedily, and mewled as he unzipped his pants, pulled out his cock, and hastily maneuvered it into her. She threw back her head and screamed as he thrust into her

Marilyn Baron

warmth again and again, like savages, until they both came. Exhausted, they collapsed on top of each other.

"Screw you, Tack," Abby growled.

"I think you just did."

There was no way he was going to get the last word.

"Now let me out," Abby ordered. Tack unlocked the car doors, opened the driver's side door, and lifted her out. Trying to maintain a modicum of dignity, she pulled up her panties, pulled down her dress, and somehow managed to stay upright on her extraordinarily high heels. When she tried to walk away, her hips swayed with a crooked tilt.

"Wait. You forgot something." Tack handed Abigail her clutch through the driver's side window. She walked away with her head held high, attempting to make a dramatic exit.

Although she wasn't Southern, she looked back at him and drawled, "Y'all's car needs a tune-up. Thanks for mine."

Giggling, and not waiting for his reply, she fumbled in her bag for her keys, switched off the alarm, and limped into her house.

The last noise she heard was the spiteful roar of Tack's engine revving up frantically as if for a qualifying round at the Daytona Motor Speedway.

And with that, Abby closed the door, the book, and the chapter on Tack Garrity.

Chapter Nine

Tack stomped into the house like a raging bull stampeding the medieval streets of Pamplona. Then he proceeded to pace the length of his foyer. He needed to calm down. He needed a drink. He wanted to scream. He desperately felt like throwing something. He'd thought about calling Aidan to come over and talk it out, but he knew Aidan was trying to get it on with his new lady, Natalie. He hoped that date was going better than the one he had just been on.

Tack took off his jacket and pulled off his shirt, tossing both on the floor, then loosened his belt. He walked over to the bar and poured himself a drink.

He was a reasonable man. Rational and calm. But damn! That Abigail Longley—she had a vicious temper, and she'd lashed out at him like a viper. So what if he deserved it? He'd attacked her like a rutting bull with no regard to whether she was willing. He'd gone off half-cocked—no, fully cocked—and he'd forgotten to pull out the condom or pull out in time. The last time that had happened, the last time he had lost his senses with a woman, was with Renata, and she had become pregnant with Isabella. You'd think he would have learned his lesson. But God, he wanted Abigail so much that, like an animal in heat, he had taken what he wanted. Because he'd lost control. *Try a little tenderness, why don't you, Tack?*

Abigail had responded to his advances, but this was not how he'd envisioned the night would end. He'd imagined waking up tangled in the sheets with Abigail in a soft bed, her bed, taking his time with her, sinking into her like he was diving into a cool spring, and surfacing to see that face, that lovely face, and losing himself in her perfect body.

Instead, she'd stomped off and said she never wanted to see him again. How had that happened? Okay, maybe he had moved too fast, but he was ready, more than ready, and she was hot and ready, too. He knew women, and unless he'd seriously misread the signals, she'd wanted him, but he should have taken a step back, taken it slower, like his father had advised.

But now it was too late. He'd blown it. Oh, it couldn't be over. He couldn't give up. Somehow, he had to get her back. But how the hell was he going to accomplish the impossible? There had to be a way. *Pull your head out of your ass, Tack Garrity, and think.*

Sprawled on the couch, his cold drink balanced on his bare stomach, his clothes strewn everywhere, it came to him. Isabella!

Chapter Ten

The women gathered at breakfast early to get a jump-start on the new day. A day that would bring them twenty-four hours closer to the gallery opening.

"Aidan's people are already removing the sawdust," said Natalie. "We should be able to complete the interior in the next few days. Then we can start hanging the artwork. The frames are all ready."

"And how was your *business meeting* with Aidan last night?" Abby teased.

"Oh, it went surprisingly well," Natalie admitted.

"Is that why he's fast-tracking the project?" Victoria said.

Natalie blushed.

"He certainly is moving fast," Abby agreed. "I noticed you never made it home last night."

"And how would you know I never came home?" Natalie inquired. "Were you waiting up for me?"

"I came home early and went looking for you. I've always wondered what an architect's house looks like."

"It's amazing. He's amazing. I think I'm in love."

"That's wonderful," said Abby.

"But I'm afraid when the job is over he'll move on. It's just that we've been working so closely together, and maybe it's just proximity, or maybe he feels obligated because I'm the client."

"I've seen the way he looks at you," said Victoria.

"It's gone beyond proximity and obligation."

"It's taken me five years to open up, and if this turns out not to be real, I'm going to be hurt all over again."

"Don't expect the worse," Abby said. "I've known Aidan a long time. He's a good guy. Where's Jane this morning?"

"You know Jane. She wants to make sure all her paintings are ready, so she's working overtime."

"I notice she's spending a lot of time with that artist, Ethan Logan," Abby said.

Natalie crunched a piece of bacon and took a bite of her omelet. "They're together day and night. She is totally crushing on him. She doesn't have much experience with men. I mean, she's a virgin—or least she was. I hope he doesn't hurt her. But how much do we really know about this guy? We know he's a talented artist, but other than that, is he good enough for Jane?"

Abby shrugged and grabbed a piece of bacon. "Victoria, what about Mr. Waterbury? How did the dinner go last night?"

Victoria's face was flushed.

"Not you too."

"He's really not as bad as we thought. I mean, I know he's trying to take *Portrait of Venus*, but he told me the whole story about that poor family, the one the painting belonged to. Joshua is just trying to do his job."

"Oh, it's Joshua now," Abby teased. "What did he tell you?"

"He told me the story of Benjamin, the Auschwitz survivor, the only one left of his family. That painting meant a lot to him. He said the woman in the picture, Venus, or rather Botticelli's model, Simonetta, looked exactly like his mother, the one who was killed in the concentration camp. It's for that reason he wanted to get it back. His father was a wealthy banker who bought the picture from an Italian art dealer for their engagement. He used to call his wife Venus, and that picture was a symbol of their great love. When they saw what was happening in Germany, they were going to sell that picture to get enough money to escape. And then, before they could make arrangements, they got home one day and found this Nazi officer had moved in and taken over their home and all their possessions. They couldn't sell the painting, and they were all shipped off to Auschwitz. Benjamin and his two younger sisters, too. When they got off the train, they were separated, and he never saw his family again. He's been trying to track down that painting since the end of the war. He just wants to see his mother's face once more."

"What a tragic story. You know, Louis used to tell me I looked like the Venus in the painting at the Uffizi Gallery."

"You totally do, Abby," Victoria agreed. "The woman in that portrait could be you. It's spooky how much it looks like you. Zach used to call me his goddess of love. And it's eerie how that portrait connects us. It was supposed to be the centerpiece of our gallery. What will we do when we lose it? Imagine! We had a genuine Botticelli masterpiece right here."

"Much as I hate to lose her, I'm glad Benjamin is going to be compensated for his loss," Abby said. "I'm still waiting for Brandon to get back to me about the authenticity of the claim, but everything seems to support Mr. Woodbury's—er, *Joshua's*—claim. Victoria, what about that picture on our Web site? It's part of our identity. And *Portrait of Venus* is all over the masterpiece cards we're printing to sell in the gift shop."

"I talked to Joshua about it, and he said if we add a line to the description label of the portrait, giving credit to the *Galleria degli Uffizi*, we have the museum's permission to use it. They're very grateful that the portrait will be back in Italian hands."

"So tell us more about Joshua. Is he married?"

"No, he travels all around the world authenticating art and trying to win restitution for victims of the Holocaust. He said he will stay in Lobster Cove until the opening, which gives me just a few weeks to find out if there's something there. I hated that man until I met him, after all."

Victoria paused. "Now it's your turn on the hot seat, Abby. How did the dinner go with your hunky cruise tour captain?"

Abby frowned. "I don't really want to talk about it."

"Sorry, now you've piqued our interest," Victoria said. "You have to talk about it."

"I got home early, and none of you were home. Let's just say Tack is not my type. End of story."

"There's more you're not telling us," Natalie accused. "Was it because of the chemistry? Did the captain's kisses leave you cold?"

"Oh, there was chemistry all right. Too much chemistry. He overstepped."

"Did he attack you?" Victoria asked, placing her

hand to her throat.

"Let's just say we attacked each other."

"Don't stop there," Natalie insisted. "Where exactly did this encounter take place?"

"In his car in the driveway."

"You couldn't wait until you got upstairs?"

"It all happened so fast—and then it was over. And now we're over."

"Honey, I'm sorry," Victoria said.

"I'm not. Tack and I are like oil and water. Louis and I never fought, but Tack and I spent the entire night sparring."

"That's called attraction," Natalie said. "If you weren't attracted to him, you wouldn't bother to fight with him."

"Did he use protection?" Victoria wanted to know.

Abby recalled the events of the previous evening. "He went from zero to sixty in one second flat, so no, but it doesn't matter. I'm infertile. Louis and I tried to conceive for five years. We tried everything, and nothing worked. I have a built-in birth control system. Enough talk about Tack Garrity. We need to get to work. Victoria, I want to review the marketing materials and the invitation list for the opening. And Natalie, if you can tear yourself away from Aidan, could you check with Chef about the food for the event? Our theme will be international, since we're going to feature art from around the world. As unsuccessful as my evening with Tack was, tell Chef to check out a new restaurant called the Crow's Nest. I understand they do catering, and the food was fabulous."

"Right."

The doorbell chimes went off.

"I'll get it," Abby said.

When she opened the door, her jaw dropped.

"Isabella?"

"Abigail!" she cried and threw herself against Abby, wrapping her arms around Abby's legs.

"Hi, honey. What are you doing here so early in the morning? Don't you have school?"

"No, silly, it's Saturday."

Abby looked at the circular driveway and saw Tack's BMW crawl down toward Hidden Cove Drive—Tack slinking away like a slimy coward.

"Did your daddy drop you off?"

"Yes, he has a 'scursion today, and I asked if I could visit you, and he said he thought that was a great idea. Grandma said Daddy is a horse's ninny."

"Well, I'd have to agree with your Grandma. How did your daddy know I'd be home?"

"He called the Archie Tek, and he told him."

"Oh, your daddy knows Aidan Ames?"

"Yes, he's Daddy's best friend."

"Of course he is." Abby fumed. Now Tack was spying on her and using her as a babysitter without even asking her permission. Like he didn't ask her permission in the car last night. That's just the kind of guy he was. Did he hope to get to her through Isabella? He knew the child was her weak spot. *Damn you, Tack Garrity.*

"Are you and my daddy having a fight?"

Abby shrugged. "Did he tell you that?"

"He's just sad. He said he made a big mistake."

Abby shook her head. *Now he regrets hooking up with me. It's a little late for that.*

"Well, honey, come on in. Have you eaten breakfast yet?"

"Yes, Grandma made me pancakes."

"Oh, that's nice. You've already been to Grandma's house this morning?"

"We live with Grandma."

Abby rolled her eyes. Tack had to be poorer than she'd thought if he lived with his mother. Well, she'd just heard on TV that one of every three young people lives with their parents. It was a sign of the times. Although you'd think that someone Tack's age, with a child, might have ventured out on his own. Instead of driving a little boat around the bay looking for whales.

Abby looked at Isabella. She was wearing her tutu again, and it was on inside out.

"This was my Mommy's. She was a ballerina. I wear it all the time."

"Yes, I noticed that. You know, later today you and I are going to go on a shopping trip into town. I'm going to get you some pretty new clothes. Would you like that?"

Isabella clapped her hands. "Yes, I love to shop, but Daddy doesn't like shopping."

"Okay, now, come on in and meet my friends."

Abby took Isabella's hand and walked her into the kitchen.

"Everyone, this is Isabella Garrity."

Everyone gathered around Isabella and fussed over her as she announced, "My name is *Queen* Isabella, and I'm going to marry The Prince of Whales."

"I think he's already taken, sweetheart," said Victoria, patting Isabella on the head.

"Not that Prince, the Prince of Whales, like the

107

whales in the ocean."

"Oh," said Natalie. "You are adorable."

"What a beauty," agreed Natalie, touching Isabella's sun-kissed ringlets.

"How long are you staying with us?" Abby wanted to know.

"Daddy said I could stay all day."

"Well, isn't that wonderful." Abby blew out a breath. "You can follow me around today and be my shadow."

"What's a shadow?"

"A little helper."

Isabella flashed a smile and danced around like a ballerina. "I'm going to be a shadow."

Jane wandered into the kitchen. "Who do we have here?"

"This is Isabella Garrity, Tack's little girl," Abby said. "Otherwise known as Queen Isabella."

"Oh!" Jane's face lit up. "I have to paint her." She turned to Isabella. "May I paint you?"

Isabella looked up at Abby with a smile. "Would that be okay?"

"Of course. That's a great idea, Jane. Isabella, why don't you follow Miss Jane up to her studio, and she'll have you sit for her while she paints your picture. Make sure you two avoid the construction site in the gallery. It's still a mess."

Jane took Isabella's hand, and they left the room chatting together.

"Now, what's that all about?" Victoria asked. "I thought you said you and Tack had a falling out."

"We did."

"Well, then, what's she doing here? Are you

babysitting?"

"I had no idea she was going to show up. I saw Tack sneaking down the driveway when I arrived at the door. He knows how much I love that child, and he's using her to get to me."

"How did he know you'd even be here?" asked Natalie.

"Your *boyfriend* told him. Apparently, he and Aidan Ames are best friends."

"Sorry, I didn't realize that," Natalie apologized. "Men and their secrets."

"No problem. She is the cutest thing. I don't mind her being here. In fact, I'm going to take her shopping for some new clothes later this afternoon. Her mother is dead, and Tack apparently has no taste and no money. He lives with his mother."

"Wow!" Victoria's face registered the correct amount of surprise.

"He can barely make ends meet," Abby added. "I feel sorry for him, but he's still a bastard."

"Come on, while Jane has her occupied, let's try to get as much done as we can," Victoria advised. "I have everything laid out in the study."

In a few steps down the hall, Abby and Victoria were there.

"Where's the *Portrait of Venus*?" asked Abby, alarmed when she didn't see the painting on the easel.

"Oh, I let Joshua borrow it. He and your lawyer, Brandon Fairbanks, are going over the contracts right now."

"Okay, but I don't even have it insured yet. If the provenance is as impeccable as I think it is, that painting is worth millions, it may even be priceless, and

I didn't even realize it. Imagine, discovering a lost Botticelli. It has to be protected."

"I totally trust Joshua."

"Of course you do. Is that your head talking, or your heart, or something in a lower region?"

Victoria blushed. "Abby!"

"Look, I totally understand lust. I got carried away last night too. There are too many hormones circulating around this house. And I think we're all choking on them. Okay, hormones aside, what are we going to do to avoid losing out, with all this work you've done publicizing *Portrait of Venus*? After the opening, we won't even have the painting in our possession. Maybe we should start over again, and I could substitute one of the Old Masters in the Longleys' private collection as our signature piece. What do you think?"

"But the *Portrait of Venus* is critical to our gallery," Victoria reminded. "It encapsulates our brand, not to mention that the model could be your twin sister."

"I know. I was so taken by that piece, and I bought it specifically to display at the entrance to the gallery. It will attract so much attention."

"I'm not worried," Victoria said. "I have a plan in mind, so let's move on to other things. I still have some bugs to work out on the Web site, but it will definitely be up and running by the opening. Clients will be able to browse our site, and it will be easy for them to make a purchase. Getting pictures of all the artwork framed and loaded onto the site before the opening is going to be tough. I also want visitors to be able to get a panoramic view of the gallery from the Web site. I have all the press releases ready for your approval. And here's the VIP guest list and the media list. The furniture and statuary will be delivered first thing in the morning. We're going to spend tomorrow moving in the furniture and the next few days hanging the artwork. Aidan is going to be directing us. Then the photographer is due to come in for the photo shoot."

Abby studied all the material Victoria showed her, then reviewed and signed off on the guest lists and the press releases.

"I know I told you to invite Tack, Isabella, and Tack's mother, but please remove them from the list."

"I'll do that."

"Victoria, this is an amazing amount of work you've put into this. Without you, we could never have launched this gallery properly. I know we have bugs to work out, but we're getting close, really close. I'm so proud of all of us."

"Jane has been working extraordinarily hard. She's painted some spectacular pieces."

"She's so secretive. She won't allow me up in the studio, so I haven't seen anything."

"Well, prepare to be dazzled. She is as talented as any of the Impressionists. Not only is she an original, but you've seen her reproductions. They are just as amazing. Perfect for people who want to own a little piece of history. And Ethan Logan's paintings of Southern scenes are breathtaking. I think those two inspire each other. Ethan is a great framer, too. He has a good eye, so he'll be very helpful."

"I have seen his work, and I think people are going to love it. I'm going to intersperse some of my in-laws' artwork just for decoration. They won't be for sale, but I will have all the Longley pieces on display around the gallery."

"Oh, and bad news about rescheduling a meeting with Val McKinley for the gallery manager position. Of all the resumes I've seen, she is the best qualified, at least on paper, but I got back in touch with her and found out more about the accident she was in. Apparently, it was that trolley by the park, the one that comes into town and then continues out to Martin Lighthouse. She was about to catch it to the gallery for her appointment with you when a little boy ran in front of it, and Val grabbed him and pushed him out of the way—and was hit by the trolley. That's why she was late. She was all bruised up, her clothes were ruined, and she was in shock. It wasn't a bad accident, just some road rash. But now she has the impression that we think she's unreliable. And since then, she's gone to work for the father of the child she saved, as his nanny. So, I guess Val is out."

"That's a shame. I admit I didn't think very highly of her when she didn't show up for the interview or call, but under the circumstances, I can understand why she didn't. And I'm glad she's okay and that the child is safe. Why don't you give her a call and say we're still interested if she can make it at some future date, and maybe she can come in and see the gallery and meet us. Maybe she'll fall in love with the Venus Gallery. Meanwhile, I think between the four of us we can manage the main gallery here at the Longley location after our reception and soft opening, and since the Maple Avenue annex won't officially open for a few more weeks, we can wait to fill that position. All of us are going to be pretty hands-on at both locations for a while at least, so it should work out. Let's keep our fingers crossed she'll have a change of heart."

"I'll give her a call," Victoria said, as she gathered up her files and hugged Abby. "I can't believe it's really happening. When you first proposed this idea in Italy, I don't think any of us thought it was real, but we've done it. My daughter, Emma, is coming from New York for the opening. She'll be a big help."

"That's wonderful. I can't wait to meet your daughter. Maybe I can set her up with that cute Caleb Reardon, the chef at the restaurant where we ate last night. I think they're about the same age, and what woman wouldn't want a man who knows his way around a kitchen? Talking about daughters, I'd better go up and find out what's happening with Tack's."

"I think Jane is probably treating Isabella to a studio-style lunch up there, so why don't you and I get a snack, and then you can take Isabella shopping this afternoon."

"Sounds wonderful. Chef's snacks are meals in themselves. And why is it no one wants me to go up to Jane's studio? Is this some kind of conspiracy?"

"Nope," Victoria said nonchalantly. "It's just that I know how busy you are."

"Too busy to ride the elevator up to the third floor?"

Victoria grabbed Abby's elbow and led her into the kitchen. "I'm starving. Let's eat. I'll be back in a minute."

"Okay, great," said Abby. "I can hardly wait to take Isabella shopping. I've been waiting my whole life to take my little girl on a shopping spree. But I have to keep reminding myself she's not mine."

"Don't be sad, Abby. Just look forward to the great

afternoon you're going to have with her and try not to think about what a pig her father is. But, before Isabella comes down, I'm dying to know. How was the sex with Tack Garrity?"

Abby rubbed her lower lip with her forefinger. "I hate to admit it, but it's the best I've ever had in a long time, maybe ever, even though it was rushed and in the front seat of a cramped car. But it was like we were both love-starved. We just pounced on each other. Like animals in a jungle. It wasn't about love. It was more about raw need."

"Is that the way it was with your husband?" Natalie asked.

Abby said quietly, "Tack Garrity is nothing like Louis. Not in any way. Louis was gentle and supportive and kind. And sex with Louis was tame. Tack is like this big brute of a brontosaurus who doesn't mean to be destructive, but still he tramples on everything in his path and takes whatever he wants."

"So you don't welcome his advances," Victoria said.

"Oh, well, there are other fish in the sea—or, as Tack might say, other whales in the pod."

"What about that cute-looking attorney, Brandon Fairbanks?"

"Brandon is married, with three kids—happily married. And I'm not looking for a man. If it happens, it happens. It's only been a year since I lost Louis. And he was one in a million. There will never be another man like him."

Chapter Eleven

Abby pulled her green Jaguar into her private parking space directly in front of the Venus Gallery shop, located only two doors down from Hazeltine's Department Store. Hazeltine's had a children's department, a specialty boutique she'd been visiting on and off ever since she and Louis first decided to have children.

She walked around to the passenger side of the car, unhooked Isabella's seat belt, helped her out, and then locked the car as they walked hand in hand toward Hazeltine's.

"So did you enjoy the morning with Miss Jane?"

"Yes, she is a good artist. She said she'd teach me to paint, too. She looked at my drawing and said I have talent. She doesn't need me to pose for her anymore. She says she's going to work on the picture while we're gone and give it to me in a frame in a few days."

"I know you're going to love the picture. I can't wait to see it."

As they passed the display window, they admired its seasonal montage of selected merchandise, and then the overhead bell above the single glass door tinkled when they opened it.

Inside Hazeltine's, they took the elevator up to the second floor. Abby had already made up her mind. One thing she had was an endless supply of money. Since

Tack had none and apparently took no interest in how Isabella looked when she went out in public, Abby was going to take matters into her own hands.

The Pink Lobster occupied a spacious corner of the second floor inside Hazeltine's, decorated with pink lobsters, lobster traps, shovels, and a fish net suspended from the ceiling. It was part of Hazeltine's but was set apart as a special shop within the store. The boutique's manager stocked the department with designer children's clothing, some of the cutest Abby had ever seen. Over the years, she'd bought baby gifts from the Pink Lobster for her friends who had children.

All she'd ever wanted was a little girl of her own to dress up. But after years of trying, it became obvious it was never going to happen. She had so much love to give a child, but motherhood didn't seem to be in the stars for her.

When she'd first met Isabella, the child was like her dream come true. If she were ever to have a child, she'd want her to be just like Isabella. The way she looked, the way she talked, the way she acted, the color of her hair. Like that song "She's Not There" by The Zombies.

"Okay, Isabella, let's shop 'til we drop."

Isabella laughed hysterically at that, while Abby took her hand and found a saleslady.

"This young woman needs a whole new wardrobe. Can you help us?"

"Of course." The girl bent down to Isabella's level.

"What a beautiful daughter you have," the salesgirl commented.

Abby flinched. "Oh, she's not mine. She's—"

"Sorry," the girl apologized to Abby and turned to

the child. "What's your name?"

"Isabella."

"That's a beautiful name. I'm Casey. What's your favorite color?"

"Pink," stated Isabella.

"Well, you're in luck, because we have a lot of pink clothes in the shop." She looked at Isabella's tutu. "Very interesting."

Abby interceded. "That was her mother's, so she likes to wear it, but I think Isabella would agree to leave it off while we're trying on new clothes."

Isabella nodded.

Abby breathed a sigh of relief. "Okay, let's get started."

Casey showed them a selection of casual clothing—colorful tees, jeans, shorts and blouses, swimwear—all designer labels, and then she brought out a collection of fancy dresses. In the past, when Abby had shopped at the Pink Lobster, she had dealt with the manager. She'd never seen this salesgirl before. Casey was young and very attractive, with her blonde hair cinched back in a ponytail. Very bright and bubbly and knowledgeable about her inventory.

Abby picked up a beautiful sparkly silver bag with a shoulder strap. "Isabella, what about this darling purse to go with your outfits? Oh, and Casey, do you carry shoes, too?"

"We have everything a little girl's heart could desire. Let me show you."

Isabella flitted around the department, pointing to this outfit and that. By the time they were through shopping, Abby and Isabella had gone through the department like a swarm of locusts and thinned out the shop's merchandise considerably. Abby had stacks of shopping bags to carry home.

"Would you like these delivered somewhere?" Casey asked.

Abby hesitated. She didn't even know where Tack lived, or rather where Tack's mother lived, and she doubted Isabella could recite the address. "Um, it's going to the home of a Mrs. Garrity, but I must admit I have no idea what the address is."

"Tack Garrity?" said Casey, turning to Isabella. "Are you Tack's daughter?"

"Yes," answered Isabella.

"You know Tack?" Abby asked.

"Everyone in Lobster Cove knows Tack. I dated him for a while, but he never introduced me to his daughter. He's pretty protective of her. You want these bags sent over to the Garrity house?"

"Yes, that would be nice. You know where it is?"

"Sure."

A streak of jealousy crept into Abby's consciousness. So Tack had dated this Barbie look-alike. And she'd been to his house. So what? If that was his type…

Pulling herself together, Abby managed, "Where does he live?"

"On Hidden Cove Drive."

"Hidden Cove Drive? That's impossible. I live on Hidden Cove Drive."

"What a coincidence."

"I mean, he couldn't live on that road. All of the homes on that road are mansions."

"It's the Garrity mansion on Hidden Cove Drive. He lives at the end of the road, in the three-story pink stucco house."

Abby shook her head. "I know that house. But no, you must be thinking of a different Garrity. This is Tack Garrity. He lives with his mother. He captains the boat that takes passengers out whale watching."

"Well, sure. We're talking about the same person. Tack only takes the boat out in his spare time. It has sentimental value. It was his dad's boat, and now his dad is in a nursing home, so he likes to keep his hand in. It makes him feel closer to his dad. And his mother lives with him. That mansion is big enough to house the whole town. It's one of the biggest houses in Lobster Cove, besides Longley House and the McClintock and Morgan mansions."

Abby's hand flew to her head. Her brain was hammering. She was so angry she felt sure she could feel the steam pouring out of her ears. That rat bastard was rich, damn him. And all this time he'd played the pauper and played her for a fool. She had bought Isabella all these clothes when he could easily afford to buy out the store if he wanted to.

"Just what does Tack do for a living?" Abby inquired evenly.

"Oh, Tack? He's an investor."

"Really," Abby said, biting her bottom lip until it nearly bled. Well, she'd already paid for the clothes. How was she going to explain it to Isabella if she changed her mind? And Isabella loved everything she'd tried on. Tack might have money, but he had no taste or scruples. The child still needed—and deserved—good clothing.

"Please deliver them all to the Garrity home, and thank you for the information."

Abby picked up her purse, offered her hand to Isabella, who took it happily, and left the store. She'd promised to take Isabella for an ice cream sundae, and she didn't want to disappoint the girl. But she was seething inside and couldn't wait to confront Tack about his deception. She pumped Isabella for information on the way to the ice cream shop.

"When did your daddy say he was going to pick you up this afternoon?" Abby asked sweetly, eager for a showdown.

"I'm supposed to call him when I'm ready to come home," Isabella said.

"After we get our ice cream, I think we'll surprise Daddy, since I know where he lives now," Abby said, struggling to keep her emotions in check.

At the ice cream shop, Abby tapped her shoe anxiously against the black-and-white checkered flooring, hardly touching her butterscotch sundae, while Isabella finished her hot fudge sundae, "with sprinkles on it."

"This was the best day ever," said Isabella as they were about to leave the ice cream shop. "Thank you for the clothes, Abigail"—Isabella hugged Abby tightly— "and the ice cream sundae. I love you."

Abby's heart expanded, and she hugged Isabella and kissed her softly on the crown of her yellow curls.

"I love you, too," said Abby, tears glistening in her eyes.

She buckled Isabella into her seat, and they drove out of town, onto Hidden Cove Drive, and past Longley House, until they got to the humongous pink stucco at the end of the road.

She parked and helped Isabella out of the car.

"I can't wait to show Daddy my new clothes. When did the lady say they'd get here?"

"Probably within the hour. And I can't wait until you show Daddy your new clothes," Abby agreed, her heart in overdrive.

"When can we play again?"

"Well, let me talk to your Daddy. You still have to view your portrait. So as soon as Miss Jane finishes it, I'll call and we'll make a plan."

"Goodie."

Abby strode purposefully up the pavement to the front of the house and pressed the doorbell several times, hoping to annoy Tack.

Tack came to the door, barefoot, in ripped jeans and a snug T-shirt, holding a paint brush. Abby's eyes bulged. He looked much more tempting than the butterscotch ice cream sundae she'd just half eaten, but she wasn't going to think about his body.

"What are you doing here? I told Isabella to call and I'd pick her up."

"I was meaning to ask you the same thing. Hidden Cove Drive? Seriously? You live down the street from me, and you forgot to mention it? You forgot to mention that you live in a mansion? You forgot to mention you were dropping Isabella off to spend the day, too—but I entirely loved the time with her, by the way."

Tack must have expected trouble was brewing. "Isabella, go find Grandma. She has your snack waiting. I need to talk with Miss Abigail, alone."

Isabella skipped down the foyer, the long black-and-white marble foyer, blissfully unaware of the tension between the two adults.

Abby tried to tamp down some of her anger, or at least dial it down to simmer, but she wasn't succeeding. She reached over and pulled Tack over the threshold by his T-shirt and out the door.

"Okay, buster, start talking."

"What do you mean?" Tack placed the paintbrush at an angle by the door.

"Nice touch."

"What."

"That paintbrush. Let me guess. You like to do your own painting."

"I'm not a slug. Just because I can afford help doesn't mean I can't work around my house. I like working with my hands."

Abby recalled just how much he liked to work with his hands. Which brought back flashes of Tack's large hands on her breasts, driving her out of her mind.

"You led me to believe you're some poor captain of a ship that's about to go under if you don't save it. Dressed in your overalls and rubber boots. And you live with your mother, but you failed to mention your mother lives with you. In a mansion. And that your poor motherless daughter doesn't wear mismatched clothes because she can't afford them but because you have no idea how to dress a child."

Tack took a step back. "Wait a minute. I never told you I was poor. You jumped to that conclusion."

"I should have known when you took me to that swanky restaurant. I thought you'd spent your last paycheck paying for those fancy clothes and those Italian shoes and that expensive meal, you bastard. You made me feel sorry for you."

Tack laughed.

"You think that's funny?"

"Well, yes."

"And I suppose you're going to tell me you own that restaurant."

Tack looked down sheepishly at the paved driveway. "I'm an investor."

"Tell me this, Tack Garrity. How did you make your money?"

Tack rubbed his chin. "I have a gift for making money. But I can see where you might have misunderstood my circumstances."

"Misunderstood?" Abby screamed, beyond control. "Misunderstood? You flat-out lied to me, Tack. And then, and then—" Abby paused to catch her breath before she could speak coherently. "Then you drop your daughter off, unannounced, and expect me to take care of her all day, as if I have nothing else to do. Who does that?"

"You said you liked kids. I thought that would make you happy."

"You were using Isabella to get to me. Well, it worked. She got to me. The only problem is that I can't stand the sight of her father."

Abby turned away and then circled back. "And when you said you knew Louis at Harvard, was that a lie, too?"

"Of course I knew Louis. I knew him very well. Lobster Cove is a small town. But we went to Harvard together, and we did a lot of business together."

"And were you ever planning to tell me that?"

"Eventually, once you got to know me."

"And, you played me. I took you on a tour of Longley House because you implied you'd never been there before, that you wanted to see how the other half lives. You've probably been in that house dozens of times."

Tack averted his eyes.

"Look at me, Tack Garrity. Why would you lie to me?"

Tack folded his arms and tapped his foot on the pavement. "Simple. My wife married me for my money. In fact, she got pregnant under false pretenses so I would have to marry her. So I promised myself I'd be careful next time I—"

"Attacked a woman in your BMW?"

"Was *attracted* to a woman. And you may as well get your story straight. You weren't exactly fighting me off."

Abby groaned, remembering how desperate she must have seemed in her eager response to Tack's advances. Turning to leave again, she reconsidered. Swirling around, she slapped Tack with the full force of her rage, right in the face, leaving a reddening imprint of her hand across his cheek.

Tack grabbed Abigail, pulled her roughly toward him, and kissed her until she lost her breath. She tried to escape from his arms, but he held on tight and drove his tongue into her mouth.

"I hate you, Tack Garrity," Abby said, struggling to break free.

"You don't hate me," Tack whispered, pausing for a breath before he kissed her again, putting his whole body into it. "I'm sorry about last night. I never meant it to happen that way. I just couldn't help myself. I came on too strong."

"Do you always take what you want?" Abby,

breathless, fought with herself not to grab onto Tack to taste him again.

"Abby, please. You don't understand. I care about you. A lot. More than you know. More than I've ever cared about anyone in a long time. I can't explain last night. I can only say I'm sorry."

"Stay. Away. From. Me. I don't want to see you again. You're dangerous."

Abby broke loose from Tack's grip, strode to her car, started the engine, and peeled away to the sound of Tack calling her name.

Chapter Twelve

"Calm down, Abby," Natalie said. The women were positioned around the kitchen table. Abby was shaking, and her teeth were chattering.

"What happened?" Victoria asked. "Where's Isabella?"

"I dropped her off at Tack's house."

Jane rearranged the flowers Tack had brought the night before. "I thought you didn't know where he lived."

"I didn't. But I found out when I had the clothes I bought for Isabella delivered. And guess where the lying son of a bitch lives? I'll tell you where he lives. He lives right down the street from us at the end of Hidden Cove Drive."

"Does he live in a guest cottage or something?" Jane asked.

"No, he lives in a mansion bigger than Longley House, and apparently he's richer than God."

"How can that be?" Natalie asked.

"We're neighbors?" Victoria chimed in.

"Yep. And all this time I thought he was a poor boat captain, doing his best to make ends meet and support his daughter. I am furious. I could tear him apart. I never want to see him again. Oh, God, I've gone and fallen for him. Shit."

"Don't cry," Natalie said. "He's not worth crying

over."

"Look, you don't have time to even think about Tack Garrity," said Victoria. "Our opening is in less than two weeks and we have a month's worth of work to do. So let's get to it."

Victoria grabbed Abby's hand and led her into the gallery space. The others followed.

"And now, we have a surprise for you. While you were gone shopping, we were busy beavers, and we got a lot accomplished."

Victoria opened the door to the gallery and swept her hand before her.

"Oh, my God. When did you do all this?"

"Today, while you were gone. Aidan and his entire team finished the space and supervised the move-in of the furniture. *Voila!* The Venus Gallery."

"It's amazing. It's just how I pictured it. We can move in the artwork right away."

"First thing in the morning the trucks are scheduled to arrive with all the artwork, framed. Aidan and Ethan will help us hang everything, and Joshua will be here, too. He wants to set up a Skype call with Benjamin, the camp survivor, so he can see the recovered painting. He's very frail. He has agreed to sell the painting to the Uffizi, and they have agreed to let him take possession for a while before he turns it over to them. Joshua just wants you to see the look on his face when he sees the *Portrait of Venus* again."

"Wow. Just wow. I can't believe you all did this while I was out wasting my time with Tack Garrity."

"It wasn't a waste of time," Natalie reasoned. "You loved spending time with Isabella."

"That was a fantasy. Isabella is not my child and

can never be. I will never have anything further to do with Tack."

"Let's sketch out where we want to put the framed artwork," Jane suggested, "so we'll know where everything goes in the morning."

The team of friends went to work deciding where the pieces would be displayed. After a while, they ate a light dinner Chef had prepared.

"I'm beat," Abby said. "I think I'll go up to bed."

"Abby, it's only eight p.m."

"I've had a hard day. I just want to sleep."

Jane nodded. "I'm going to get Ethan to move the paintings in my studio down here tonight so we can get a jump on tomorrow. I think Abby has the right idea. Maybe we should all turn in early."

"Can't," said Natalie. "Aidan and I are going out to dinner."

"Should we wait up?" asked Jane.

"That's a big no," Natalie answered. "What about you, Victoria?"

"Well, Joshua wanted me to stop by the Sea Crest Inn, where he's staying, so we can talk about the portrait. He says hot chocolate is their specialty and that they have a Swedish cook who makes fresh Danish and pastries every morning."

"Right," said Natalie. "He wants to talk about the portrait, in his room at the Inn. And why would you be sampling the Danish and pastries unless you're planning to stay over and have breakfast in the morning?"

Victoria blushed. "They also have fireplaces all over the Inn. And a beach."

"Two more good reasons to spend the night with a

man you hardly know," Natalie teased, countering with, "but don't be too late in the morning. We have to get an early start."

The doorbell rang. Natalie went to answer it. When she returned, she wasn't smiling.

"Trouble's at the door. With a capital T. And his name is Tack Garrity. Should I send him away?"

Abby shook her head. "No, let's get this over with. The sooner I get rid of him, the better. He's like an albatross around my neck."

Natalie came back with Tack. Instead of leaving them to settle their differences in private, the women gathered around Abby in a show of solidarity.

"We need to have a conversation," Tack stated. He looked at Jane, Natalie, and Victoria and then directed his remarks to Abby. "Do they need to be here?"

"I have nothing to hide from my friends."

"All right, then. The clothes you bought Isabella were delivered."

"Did you like them?"

"That's not the point. I'm sending them back to Hazeltine's."

"What does Isabella think about that?"

"Isabella threw a tantrum, and she's not talking to me. Reminds me of her mother. I just want you to know that I'm returning the clothes you bought her. You spent thousands of dollars on my daughter. That is over the top."

"That's when I thought you were poor."

"Well, I'm not poor, and I can't allow you to do that. I can afford to buy clothes for my own child."

"Then why don't you?"

"And, if I were poor, do you know how crushing

that would be to my manhood?"

Abby glanced down at the bulge in the front of Tack's jeans. Apparently he was in a constant state of readiness. "It looks like your manhood is still intact." The girls giggled. "Why are you going to take away your daughter's pleasure? She loved trying on the clothes. She loved the idea of wearing them, and now you're taking them back? Can't you at least let her keep some of them?"

"I thought you'd be stubborn. That's why I brought this." Tack pulled out his checkbook and scribbled the amount of the purchase on a check, then signed it. He handed the check to Abby.

"I'm not going to take your money," Abby said.

"And I'm not going to take yours, so it seems we're at an impasse."

"We're not accomplishing anything here, and I'm very busy. Let me show you to the door," Abby said, stomping out in front of Tack and slamming the study door behind him.

"She's got it bad," said Natalie.

"Really bad," agreed Victoria.

"But they're fighting," Jane pointed out.

"That's what people do when they're in love," reasoned Natalie.

****

Abby looked out at the ocean and toward Martin Lighthouse from her bedroom window. Dressed in her pajamas and fuzzy slippers, she cinched the bathrobe tighter around her waist to keep from shivering. *Damn that Tack Garrity!* From her position at the window, she could see Tack's house, all lit up. How could Isabella understand what was happening? They'd had so much fun picking out clothes. She could imagine the little girl's tearstained face when her father said she couldn't keep the outfits. She knew Tack loved his daughter, but the man had absolutely no idea how to raise her. She needed a mother's loving guidance, and she had no mother. All she had left of her mother was that turquoise tutu. If Tack didn't exert some parental control, she would be wearing the tutu to her senior prom and her wedding.

Thinking about Isabella brought tears to her eyes. For years she and Louis had tried to have children. First the regular way, then the fertilization route. And still nothing. Now Louis was gone, and all the plans they'd made, all the dreams they'd spun, had disappeared with him. When she met Tack and Isabella, her heart had swelled and she had taken the child in, and now she couldn't bear to let her go. And as much as she *didn't* want to think about Tack, she couldn't *stop* thinking about him—his kisses, his hands, his mouth on her breasts, his powerful body invading hers. Memories of their coupling in the car were keeping her up at night, keeping her tossing and turning and panting. She wanted to feel his hot breath on her face and his wet mouth on her lips. And she wanted to feel him inside her again.

Frustrated, she closed the drapes and burrowed under the covers. Her last thoughts before she drifted off to sleep were of Tack.

Chapter Thirteen

Abby woke refreshed and ready to seize the day.
Dealing with Tack last night had been exhausting, but
today was the culmination of her dreams for the new
gallery. All the planning and hard work was about to
pay off. She dressed in a pair of straight-legged jeans
and pulled a blue-striped linen Eileen Fisher top over
her head. Then she put on a pair of socks and sneakers
and went downstairs.

As usual, Chef had laid out a scrumptious spread,
and she was starving. She took a plate from the table
and filled up on the buffet—eggs, bacon, waffles, the
works.

Her housemates drifted in, one by one, yawning.

"Up late, girls?" Abby asked eventually. "Or in
early?"

None of them would meet her gaze.

"That's okay. Just because everyone in this room
had sex last night but me…"

"You're the one who doesn't want to have sex with
Tack," said Victoria. "Personally, I wouldn't throw him
out of my bed."

"That's enough talk about sex and Tack Garrity,
and don't mention either of those two thoughts in the
same breath again, at least not in my presence,"
cautioned Abby. "Have the paintings arrived?"

Natalie did a sitting version of the happy dance.

"Delivered as promised. We had them unload the crates in the gallery. We checked that the frames were all to your specifications. They're all ready to be hung. And may I just add that I think Tack Garrity is very well hung."

"No, you may not," said Abby. "Keep your opinions to yourself."

"Just sayin','" Natalie answered, fairly skipping into the gallery ahead of Victoria, Jane, and Abby.

The four ran around the room like delighted schoolgirls, stopping to inspect each painting.

Ethan, Aidan, and Joshua were standing by with hammers and picture hooks, a hot-looking cavalcade of men, ready to be directed. She was sure if she called Tack he'd rush right over with his toolkit, too, but this was *her* life, and Tack wasn't a part of it.

Abby glanced at Ethan. "Let's start with your paintings. The ones you brought from South Carolina and the ones you've painted of Lobster Cove since you arrived."

The guys ambled over to Ethan's stack of paintings and, consulting their plans, started hanging the artwork.

"Ethan, you are just brilliant," Abby gushed. "I knew when we saw your paintings they would be perfect for the gallery, but the new scenes of Lobster Cove are magnificent."

"Thank you, Abby. I love it here in Lobster Cove. The people are so friendly." He stared at Jane like a lovesick puppy, and Jane's adoring look mirrored his. Abby would be surprised if they hadn't slept together. They certainly spent every waking moment together. Jane might have been a virgin when she met Ethan, but Ethan was a real charmer. It wouldn't take much convincing or courting to get Jane to shed her inhibitions, along with her clothes. Her new clothes. Natalie had taken Jane shopping for a new wardrobe, as well as to Hair's the Thing, the beauty shop on Main Street, to get a new haircut and a makeover. After that, Plain Jane was nowhere to be found.

"Okay, now for Jane's paintings." Abby went to the second stack of artwork. "Her paintings go in this next room. The placement is marked on the plan."

Jane could barely contain her excitement. "My work is going to be in a gallery, my gallery," she yelped.

Slowly Jane's masterpieces filled the space. Her paintings of scenes on their cruise excursions. Paintings of scenes all over the capitals of Europe, painted from her memories of their buying trips. Paintings of Lobster Cove, which the tourists would love, and paintings from her studio window of the ocean and the Martin Lighthouse at various times of the day and a variety of light levels. Her style was reminiscent of and heavily influenced by Chagall and Monet, but her brand was her own, as was her unique visual style. Abby predicted she would be famous one day. What a coup to introduce such a talent to the world. Those paintings would fly out of the gallery. But first Abby was going to purchase one of Jane's paintings of the scene behind Longley House.

Once Jane's work was hung, the guys hung the paintings the four friends had collected from Prague, Paris, the Greek islands, and the Balearic Islands of Spain—Mallorca and Ibiza—and other places they'd visited after their cruise. All mini-masterpieces from undiscovered but hugely talented artists. They reminisced about how they'd acquired each one, recalling their conversations with the artists and remembering the fun they'd had traveling around Europe.

There was the Italian painter Michelangelo—his mother must have had a real sense of humor. They'd discovered him painting scenes of Lake Como and Portofino. Jane apparently had a thing for artists. She had developed a crush on the painter and had fallen in love with his artwork, so they had to carry his *Whispers of Portofino* painting and his breathtaking Lake Como series. After they pulled Jane away from the sexy artist and the beautiful scenery, they traveled to Prague to the Charles Bridge, where Jane walked up and down, settling on one particular quiet painter whose work she also fell in love with and that the Venus Gallery would now carry.

They discovered a Russian-born artist in Venice, painting scenes of the Grand Canal. Abby had fallen in love with *Ca' d'Oro*, of Palazzo Santa Sofia, one of the older palaces in the city, and signed the artist to a long-term contract. There was something about the way the light shone on the façade, reflecting the gold of the building and the blue of the water, that she couldn't get out of her mind. That was the beauty of art, the way it serenaded your soul.

Paris was fun, and they'd picked up some exquisite Seine River scenes from the City of Lights. Visitors would enjoy a large selection of styles, colors, and media, from oil and acrylic paintings on canvas and paper, to watercolors, embellished serigraphs on wood or canvas, lithographs, and *giclées* in color on canvas. They had acquired works directly from the artists or, if an artist was deceased, from the artist's estate. Jane still wasn't over their trip to Giverny, Monet's home. She had felt she was making a pilgrimage to the past when she stepped into the artist's studio and explored his gardens. That was the thing about Jane. She was an original, but she could deliver a faithful reproduction of any artist dead or alive. That was how she had learned to paint, by imitating the masters.

Abby's goal for the gallery was to demystify art, to bring a broad cross-section of artwork to Lobster Cove so visitors could appreciate the beauty and take home a slice of life from their travels to Lobster Cove. Whether the visitor was in the market for aesthetic beauty or was a serious collector, the Venus Gallery would have a lot to offer. After visiting the gallery, patrons could visit the sculpture garden outside and relax on one of the new benches Aidan had set facing the ocean, view the iconic Martin Lighthouse at sunset or delight in the color of the ocean and the light from the sky as it shifted during daylight hours.

The Venus Gallery would offer artwork at a range of prices. Abby had finally decided that to attract serious collectors she would sell off a selection of paintings from her in-laws' collection, including Old Masters, Impressionists, and Modern Masters. She would also display the Longley art she did not want to sell, so the world could enjoy it with her. The pieces she and her new partners had collected consisted of mostly contemporary living artists, but there was something for everyone to like, from hand-signed original Chagall drawings and paintings to artwork by Matisse and Renoir. Of course Jane would be the artist-in-residence, and it looked very likely that Ethan Logan might stay on. At least that was her hope, along with Jane's. The two had grown very close.

Abby's plan for the future was for Jane, at least, to offer painting lessons and lectures, and that the gallery would sponsor traveling exhibits. In addition, Abby planned to fly in some of the artists whose work they had collected and hold periodic signing events and meet-the-artist gatherings. Victoria had already prepared single glossy bio sheets of each artist with his or her picture.

The statuary was in place, and all the pictures were hung. Abby walked through each room, approving each piece in turn. When her tour was concluded, she covered her head with her hands and burst into tears.

"Abby, what's wrong?" Jane said, alarmed.

"Nothing's wrong. Everything is perfect. I just can't believe we did it."

The women gathered in a circle and hugged.

"We did it together," Victoria said.

"When will the gift shop be stocked?" Abby asked.

"All the inventory is in. We're going to set up the Maple Avenue location tonight."

"It looks like we're ahead of schedule," Natalie said.

Abby walked to the gallery entrance, to the windows that were visible from the driveway. "There's just one thing missing. The centerpiece, the *Portrait of Venus*."

"Joshua said the painting's new owner would allow you to keep it for the opening," Victoria reminded her.

"I know, but what about after the opening? Everything revolves around that portrait."

The women gathered around Abby. Natalie brought

her over to a comfortable couch. "Now, you need to sit down. We have a surprise for you."

Ethan and Jane left the room, and when they returned, they were each holding a framed picture and an easel. Jane placed the easel in front of the couch and placed a portrait on the easel. "This is for you, Abby."

Abby looked at the picture and burst into fresh tears.

"Don't you like it?" Jane wrung her hands.

"Like it? Jane, it's phenomenal. Did you paint this?"

"Yes, in the style of Sandro Botticelli. I used his exact technique."

"It's *Portrait of Venus*," Abby exclaimed. She got up and studied the painting closely.

"When did you paint this?"

"I did a reproduction of the original, using the actual painting as a guide. That's why I wouldn't let you into the study."

Joshua went to the painting. "This is amazing. It looks exactly like the original. Even I can't tell the difference."

Jane instructed Ethan to place the portrait in a place of honor at the gallery entrance. "Now you have your painting back."

"Jane, you are a major talent. I agree with Joshua. I can't tell the difference between this and the original. You must have worked long hours to complete this in time."

"I knew how much it would mean to you."

Abby embraced Jane. "Thank you so much. Thanks to all of you. Just think, a few short months ago we didn't even know each other, and look at us now."

"Now, stay seated, Abby," said Victoria. "Don't look yet. We have another surprise."

Jane placed a second portrait on the easel. "You can look now."

Jane opened her eyes. "Oh, Jane. Oh, I don't know what to say."

"It's Queen Isabella," Jane said, beaming.

"You painted her in the style of Diego Velázquez, posed like The Infanta Margarita in *Las Meninas* at the Prado. Her dress, her countenance, her spirit... This reproduction is magnificent, but the face—this is our Isabella. It's breathtaking. We've got to show it to her."

"I'm so glad you like it."

"She is going to love it. Tack is going to— How are we going to show it to her without Tack? I don't want to see him."

"I'll go pick her up and bring her over," said Aidan. "Tack's taken the boat out today. Isabella is home with her grandmother, so we'll sneak her over here."

"We'll have another unveiling," Abby said. "And I'll have Chef make something special for dessert as a special treat for Isabella. Jane, this is wonderful."

Thirty minutes later, Aidan escorted Isabella into the gallery. She walked around, looking at the pictures and clapped. "I love this. It's beautiful."

"Thank you, sweetheart. We worked very hard to make this dream come true. And now, we have a big surprise for you." Abby took Isabella's hand and led her to where her covered portrait was displayed on an easel.

When Isabella was directly in front of it, Jane pulled off the white cloth.

Isabella got very quiet and took in a breath. She

kept staring at the portrait. "It's me. It's me. I look like a queen."

"Or a little princess," said Jane.

"Didn't Jane do a wonderful job?" Abby prompted.

"Thank you, Miss Jane." Isabella let go of Abby's hand and gave Jane a big hug. Then she ran back to Abby.

"Thank you, Abby. I love you." She clung to Abby and wouldn't let go. Then the tears started cascading down her cheeks.

"Honey, what's wrong? Don't you like your painting?"

"Yes, but Daddy won't let me keep the clothes you bought me."

Abby bristled. Tack was infuriating. She thought by now he would have calmed down and let his daughter keep at least some of the clothes.

"My grandma says Daddy is as stubborn as an old billy goat."

Well, she's right.

"The clothes are still in the bags by the door. He says he's going to take them all back. He stomps around the house, slamming doors and barking."

"Barking?"

"Yelling for no reason. Banging pots and pans around in the kitchen, and throwing things. Grandma says he's irritable and moping around like a lovesick cow. Is my Daddy sick?"

Abby smiled to learn that Tack was suffering too. "Not in the way you think. I have an idea. Why don't you give me your tutu, and I will have it dry cleaned and preserved so it will stay beautiful always. We wouldn't want anything to happen to it. I'll give it back to you to keep in your closet. Tell your daddy you will stop wearing the tutu if he lets you keep the clothes."

"Do you think he will?"

"I have a feeling he will. Now let's go have a treat in the kitchen, and then Aidan will drive you home. Tell your grandma we will have the picture framed and sent over to your house."

Isabella removed her tutu and gave it to Abby before she took her hand, and they walked into the kitchen. Small victory.

After dessert, Aidan drove Isabella home.

"I just love that child," said Abby. "I wish—"

Everyone around the table was silent. Everyone knew what she wished.

"Okay, let's change the subject," suggested Victoria. "The photographer is due in tomorrow and will be here all day. For the rest of the week, I'll be on publicity and marketing duty, and working on launching the Web site."

"I'll be organizing the RSVPs," said Natalie. "So far, we have a full house, including media, local businesses, friends, and VIPs. The catering menu is set. That new chef, Caleb Reardon from the Crow's Nest, is handling that, under the direction of Chef. And the orchestra is set. Flowers, done. Nametags, done."

"I'll work on my opening remarks," said Abby. "Can you shoot me the updated guest list, Natalie?"

"Will do."

"It goes without saying I don't want to see Tack Garrity at this event."

"He wasn't invited, so we should be good," Natalie assured her friend.

"After the VIP event, we'll be open to the public.

We'll manage the gallery ourselves, in shifts, until we get a permanent manager hired. We'll start out with limited hours so we can handle it and still have a life. Jane, please tell Ethan to keep painting. We need a good supply of his work, and yours. I have a feeling this opening event is going to be a sellout. And let me just say I love all of you. I can't imagine what my life would have been like if I hadn't met you, if we hadn't found each other. I'm more grateful than you will ever know."

"I think I speak for all of us when I say we feel the same way about you," said Victoria.

"We can certainly be proud of ourselves and all we've accomplished," agreed Abby.

Chapter Fourteen

Tack Garrity strode into the gallery in a perfectly tailored tuxedo, looking like some movie star stepping up to accept his Academy Award. He surveyed the crowd until his eyes fixed on Abby.

Abby headed to where Tack was standing to prevent him from coming any farther into the gallery.

"You were uninvited. What are you doing here?"

"I'm Aidan's Plus One."

Abby rolled her eyes and turned away. "Well, just stay out of my way. I don't want you to create a scene. In fact, I'd prefer it if you left, now."

Tack spun her around to face him.

"You purposely dressed that way, in that see-through gauzy thing, just to tempt me," Tack accused.

"Tack, I don't dress for you. I dress to please myself. I didn't expect you to be here. In fact, I was quite sure you wouldn't be."

Tack's face transformed to molten steel. "You look like her."

"Like whom?"

"Like Venus, like the girl in the painting."

"That's the effect I was going for."

"Well, you damn well pulled it off. And it makes me want to pull this dress off you, right here, right now."

Abby blew out a breath, frustration rising like mist

on a river at dusk. Tack's caveman imitation was wearing thin. "Tack, if you don't behave yourself, I'm going to have security escort you out, although you probably own the security firm, too. I can't help it if you own every damn business in town."

"I'm an investor," Tack reminded her. "I invest in my community."

Abby shook her head. "That's very noble of you. Now do us both a favor and get out. This is my night. You're not a part of it. I won't let you spoil it for me."

Still in Tack's arms, Abby gave him a critical appraisal.

"Did you think I'd show up in overalls?"

"It crossed my mind."

"You didn't think I own a tuxedo?"

"I had no doubt you did." Abby shrugged. "You probably own a tuxedo rental shop. Why would I care?"

Tack tightened his grip. "You do care, and I'm going to prove it." Tack kissed her long and hard, and it would have knocked her off her heels if she hadn't been trapped in his arms.

Every part of her body was responding to him, but this was not the time or the place. She pulled away from his embrace and immediately missed his warmth.

"I heard Jane painted a picture of Isabella. She can't stop talking about it. I want to see it."

"It's at the framers'. Do you own them, too?"

"No, as it happens, I don't. I want to pay you for the portrait."

"Tack, you can't buy everything. That painting was a gift, because we love Isabella. We won't accept any money for it."

"Isabella told me you convinced her to retire the

tutu. I appreciate it more than you know. I hated seeing that thing on her. It reminded me of Renata."

"I did you a favor, so now will you do me one and let her keep the things I bought her?"

"My mother agrees with you, so we're keeping them. That's what I came to tell you."

"Great. Now I have to get back to my guests."

"Can we talk afterward?"

"What's there to talk about?"

"I have a lot more to say to you."

"Well, I have nothing more to say to you," said Abby. *Unless you want to talk about shared custody of Isabella.*

"I'm not going to go away unless you agree to talk to me."

"Whatever it takes. Call me this week, and we can set up an appointment."

"It's a date, then."

"Tack, you're delusional. It won't be a date."

"I'll wear my overalls, then."

Abby tried her best to look stern as she watched Tack walk out the door. She had half a mind to follow him and pummel him into oblivion. Or maybe she just wanted to touch him again. *Focus, Abigail. Focus.* Tack was a major distraction she did not need tonight.

Abby moved through the crowd. Everyone on the invitation list had shown up. Even those not on the list had shown up. Tack being a case in point. People were mingling, having fun, enjoying the food and the music, and soaking up the atmosphere. She'd received so many compliments about the design of the gallery and the variety of the artwork available. Everyone agreed the gallery was unique.

"Abigail, I love what you've done here," said the mayor of Lobster Cove. "The Venus Gallery is going to be a real boon to our town. Now people won't feel compelled to flee to Boston to get their culture fix."

"That was exactly what we had in mind. Lobster Cove will be a new travel destination."

"I saw you talking to Tack Garrity earlier," the mayor noted. "He's a fine man, don't you agree?"

Abby frowned. It seemed Tack was in the room, even when he wasn't.

"If it hadn't been for Tack, in that last economic downturn, Lobster Cove might have turned into a ghost town. He literally put us on the map, bringing in the Crow's Nest for fine dining, putting up the capital for a number of local businesses. He has his hands in everything."

And on everything, especially me, she refrained from saying.

"When Tack moved back to Lobster Cove, everything changed. We've become a much more vibrant community because of his contributions—not only his money but his time. When my term is up, I wouldn't be surprised if Tack will run for mayor. And he'll win. It would be a landslide. Almost everyone in this town owes Tack a debt of gratitude."

Why don't you erect a statue of Tack in the park?

"Well, I've got my eye on several paintings. I want to go and reserve them. Fine job, Abigail. Louis would have been proud."

"And his parents would have been horrified."

"No doubt, but this town needs new blood, new ideas, and you and Tack are right in sync."

Don't pair me with him.

"Well, I'd better circulate, Mr. Mayor. Thank you so much for coming. And we'd appreciate it if you'd encourage others to visit in the future."

"Count on it." The mayor wandered off.

Abigail tasted one of the hors d'oeuvres being passed. Delicious. She needed to compliment the chef from the Crow's Nest. Actually, the chef was engaged in conversation with Emma, Victoria's daughter, who'd flown in from New York for the event. She was a darling girl, and she and Caleb Reardon made a handsome couple. And they seemed to be enjoying each other's company immensely. It seemed unlikely Emma would have to travel all the way from New York to the small town of Lobster Cove to find a man, but evidently there was something in the water in Lobster Cove. Maybe someone should bottle it and sell it as a love potion.

Abby went over to the couple. "Caleb, your hors d'oeuvres are exceptional. Everyone was so excited your restaurant was catering. You've done a fantastic job. I hope it generates a lot of business for the Crow's Nest. Emma, I hope you're enjoying yourself."

"This is the most fun I've had in a long time. Your gallery is fabulous, and I've never seen Mom so happy. And I'm really enjoying the company." She gazed into Caleb's eyes.

"I saw you talking to Tack a while ago," said Caleb. "It's a shame he had to leave. If it weren't for Tack, I wouldn't even have a restaurant."

"I'm curious. How did you and Tack meet?"

"At Harvard. He knew I wanted to own a restaurant one day. When I invited some of my fraternity brothers and their dates over for a formal dinner one night, he raved about the food and insisted he wanted to invest in my future ventures. We're equal partners in the Crow's Nest. He's the money man. He's also invested in several of my other restaurants around the country. Tack has the Midas touch. And a heart of gold."

Abby exhaled. Tack must have a split personality. It seemed she'd only seen his worst side. "Thank you, Caleb. Well, you two have fun."

Abby wandered over to chat with some reporters and pose for some photos. Guests were clustered around Jane's paintings, raving about the next Chagall. Checkbooks and credit cards were being waved around. It looked like Natalie had her hands full taking orders.

Aidan came up to Abby. "Well, it looks like you ladies have a hit on your hands."

"Thanks to your great work with the design and buildout."

"Well, I had a lot of help from Natalie. She has a good eye for design, and she kept the project right on track."

Abby smiled. "You like her, don't you?"

"I love her, Abby. It happened so fast, but I'm really serious about the woman."

"I'm glad, Aidan. She deserves to be happy, and you are just the man to do it."

"And talk about being happy, why are you giving Tack such a hard time?"

"You and Tack talk about me?"

"He can't stop talking about you. And yes, he's my best friend, so we talk about the women we're interested in."

"Has he told you how crude he is, how he just takes what he wants? Tack has this whole town fooled.

He's nothing but a big brute, Aidan."

Aidan smiled. "Abby, he knows what he wants and he goes after it. Any woman in this town would give anything if Tack Garrity looked at them the way he looks at you. But he has his heart set on you. Look, his first wife, Renata, was a nasty piece of work. She was never in love with Tack, and she didn't give Isabella the time of day. She ripped his heart out. She was only interested in his money, and she cheated on him from the moment she married him. I hate to speak ill of the dead, but she won't be missed, except by Isabella, who really hardly knew her. That child is amazing, and she deserves better."

"Well, that's one thing we can agree on."

"She deserves a mother like you."

Abby laughed. "That's quite a stretch."

"It's not my place to say, but Tack loves you. Isabella loves you. I don't see what the problem is."

"Tack has never said he loves me. Maybe he's looking for a mother for Isabella, but—"

"It's a lot more than that, Abby. You may not be able to see it, but Tack is the best man I know. He may have made some mistakes with you, come on too strong, but his feelings for you are sincere. He's decent and strong and dependable and generous, and almost everyone in this town will tell you that."

"Now you sound like the mayor."

"Men like Tack don't come along every day, Abigail. Why don't you give him another chance?"

Abby pursed her lips. "I appreciate that you're his friend, but I don't think Tack and I are at all compatible."

"From where I sit, you're a perfect match," Aidan

said. "Well, I've left Natalie alone long enough. She could use my help. I think you may have sold out your entire inventory. Especially the Jane Nash pieces. And Ethan Logan's are a close second."

"Thanks again for everything, Aidan."

Abby stepped up to the microphone and cleared her throat. She picked up a flute of champagne and tapped her fork against the glass. Everyone in the crowd turned to her.

"Hello, and welcome. For those of you who don't know me, I'm Abigail Adams Longley, one of the owners of the Venus Gallery. I'd like to introduce you to my three partners in this exciting new venture—Jane Nash, whose paintings you've seen and enjoyed tonight, Natalie Jasper, and Victoria Dare. I don't know if you've heard the story, but we met on a cruise ship, bonded over a painting, *The Birth of Venus*, and decided to open up an art gallery. After months of hard work, we did it. We couldn't have done it without each other. Frankly, I don't know what I would do without these women. They came into my life at a time when I really needed them, when we really needed each other, and since then life's never been the same.

"It is our hope that you have found something you liked here tonight and that you'll keep coming back if for nothing else but to enjoy beautiful art. We've collected fine art from around the globe, paintings you won't get in any other gallery, artwork you can fall in love with that takes you to another place, another time, that ignites a spark in your soul. If that happens, then we've done our job. Be sure to pick up a brochure about our gallery, about the services and features we offer, and enjoy the good food and music and company. We hope you'll spread the word about the Venus Gallery. And thank you so much for coming."

Abby relieved Natalie at the register, and Natalie and Aidan walked off hand in hand outside in the moonlight, to one of the benches with a partial view of the ocean, perhaps the most romantic spot in the world. Strains of the orchestra filled the gallery and could probably be heard all the way to the sea. From the window Abby could see Natalie and Aidan kiss. Aidan spoke, and then Natalie jumped into Aidan's arms and wouldn't let go.

Abby was thrilled for them, and she wanted a love like that for herself. After Louis died, she had thought she would never experience those strong feelings again. But then she met Tack. He was gruff at times, but tonight, through the picture others painted of him, she had seen another side of Tack, another layer. Perhaps she should give him another chance.

Jane and Ethan were also walking through the gallery hand in hand. What a coup for Jane. She was the new darling of the art world, and Ethan was totally swept away by her. Plain Jane had blossomed into a beautiful flower in front of their eyes.

Joshua Waterbury couldn't keep his hands or his eyes off Victoria. Victoria, who not too long ago thought she had nothing to live for. Had she jumped off the cruise ship, she would have missed out on a whole new life. And Abby would have missed out on a wonderful friendship. Joshua lived in London and traveled around the world, but if they were in love, they would work it out. So it seemed everybody had somebody except her. Lobster Cove was a haven for lovers.

Abby's thoughts wandered back to Tack. She was certainly physically attracted to him. She had agreed to meet him once more, give him a chance to have his say, but other than that, she wouldn't see him again. One thing she'd miss about Tack was Isabella. But it was cruel to maintain a relationship with her if she wasn't going to see Tack on a permanent basis. Cruel to both Isabella and herself. Well, she had a lot to occupy her mind without thinking of Tack. The four women had each spent time at the register, talked to visitors, given tours—it had been a long day and a long evening. But they'd achieved their dream, and from now on it would be smooth sailing.

Chapter Fifteen

"Wow, what a night," Jane sighed at breakfast the next morning. "I've sold all my paintings, and so has Ethan. We need to get to work right away and paint some more."

"It was exhausting and exhilarating at the same time," agreed Natalie, whose grin was contagious.

Victoria was suspicious. "Okay, what are you hiding, Natalie?"

Natalie stuck her right hand out. "Aidan asked me to marry him. We're engaged."

The girls shrieked and lined up to give Natalie a hugs and congratulate her.

"Let me see that rock," said Abby. "Wow, that's some stone!"

"It's beautiful, isn't it," agreed Natalie, whose happiness outshone the glittering multi-carat emerald-cut diamond.

"Did you set a date?" Jane asked.

"No, Aidan just asked me last night, and with all the activity, we didn't get down to any details, just that we're in love and we want to be together forever. And I am so happy."

"We're happy for you," Abby said. "Aidan is a wonderful man."

"Listen, I hate to break up this party, but I promised to spend the day with Emma, take her around, get to know the town a little better, and that cute chef Caleb Reardon wants us to stop by his restaurant for lunch," Victoria said. "I think he just wants to spend more time with Emma. He's asked her out for tonight." She noticed Abby was unusually quiet. "Abby, what are you going to do for the rest of the day?"

Abby stared at the food on her plate and pushed the eggs around with her fork.

"You haven't eaten a thing, Abby," Jane said.

"I'm not hungry."

"Here, take my last piece of bacon," Jane said, tossing a piece of bacon onto Abby's plate. "It's crispy, just the way you like it."

Abby made a face and held up her hand. "No, no, I—I think I'm going to be sick." Abby ran to the bathroom next door and vomited. As soon as possible she ran a glass of water, took a large sip and swished it around in her mouth before spitting it out and returning to the table.

"Abby, you're white as a sheet," Natalie said. "What's wrong?"

"Nothing. It's nothing. I'm just exhausted. It's been a long couple of months."

"I'm sure that's it," said Jane. "Would you like some juice? You have to eat something."

Abby got up from the table and went toward the buffet. "I'll get it." She took a step. Her eyes glazed over and she went down, hitting her head against the sideboard.

"Abby!" Natalie screamed, rushing to her friend, who lay slumped on the floor. "Someone get a wet towel. She's bleeding! Help me lift her. Get her into my car. We're taking her to the doctor. Does anyone know who her doctor is?"

The women shook their heads.

"Does this town even have a hospital? I think it has a Family Health Clinic. Why don't we know anything about this place?"

"I'm going to call 9-1-1, get an ambulance," said Jane.

Natalie smoothed Abby's bangs back from her head. "One of you call Aidan, have him meet us here. He'll know where to go. She's perspiring. She's still unconscious. She's white as a sheet. Damn! What could be wrong with her?"

"Maybe she caught a bug last night, ate some bad food. I don't know. Everything seemed to be excellent, though." Jane picked up the phone and dialed Aidan's number.

"Aidan, it's Jane. Abby's fainted. She's bleeding. We need help. Can you get here now?" Jane turned to Natalie. "He's on his way."

Victoria came back with a wet cloth, wiped Abby's forehead, and pressed the cloth against her head to stop the bleeding.

"She's coming to," Natalie said. "Here, help me get her up and to a chair."

"What happened?" asked Abby, wobbling as her friends helped her into a kitchen chair.

"You fainted. We're taking you to the hospital."

"I don't want to go to Lobster Cove Hospital. I don't want everyone in this town to know my business. There's a hospital in Bar Harbor. But I don't need a doctor. I'm fine."

"You're not fine. You fainted. You vomited. And you're bleeding. Aidan is coming to help us."

"Don't call Aidan."

"Why not? We don't know where the doctors are, where your doctor is."

"Most of my doctors are in Boston."

"No one local? We found an OB/GYN named Lori Sato."

"No. I have my own OB/GYN in Bar Harbor, but like I told you, I don't need a doctor," Abby insisted.

The doorbell rang.

"Where's Abby?" Aidan shouted, running into the kitchen.

"Aidan, you didn't need to come out here," Abby protested. "I'm fine."

Aidan inspected Abby. "You look like a ghost. What happened?"

"She came downstairs, didn't eat any breakfast, vomited, and then fainted and hit her head on the sideboard. She needs medical attention."

"I'll be fine. Just let me sit here."

Aidan scooped Abby up in her arms. "Natalie, open the back door. I'll get her into the car, and you ride with her in the back seat."

"Everyone, stop making such a fuss. I probably have food poisoning or something."

"Jane, you ride with me," said Victoria. "We'll follow Aidan."

"Where's Abby's purse with her insurance cards?" Aidan asked.

"I think she must have left her bag up in her bedroom. I'll get it and bring it." Jane ran for the elevator.

Aidan got Abby settled in the back seat and took the wheel.

"What did you eat last night?" Natalie asked.

"What everyone else ate. None of you are sick."

"You're probably just exhausted. Maybe you caught a cold. Well, we'll just have you checked out. Abby, where's your doctor?"

"Dr. Hadley in Bar Harbor, downtown in the harbor area."

"Aidan, do you know where that is?"

"Yes. Hang on. It's only about ten miles away down the coast, but since it's downtown, traffic is slow, so maybe another ten- to fifteen-minute ride. We might have to fight for a parking space."

"This is so silly and unnecessary," Abby kept repeating.

"Let us be the judge of that," Natalie said.

They entered downtown Bar Harbor, and luckily Aidan found a parking space right in front of the doctor's office. He opened the back door of the car, scooped up Abby, and carried her in.

"For heaven's sakes, Aidan, you don't need to carry me."

"Hey, we've got an emergency here, can anybody help us?" Aidan shouted as he entered the office.

A girl came out from behind the desk.

"This is Abby Longley," Aidan explained. "She fainted and fell and, oh, yeah, she vomited. She bumped her head on the edge of a table. She's bleeding."

"You're all crazy. I'm fine. I can walk by myself."

"Carry her into this exam room," instructed the receptionist.

Aidan placed Abby on the exam table. "Now lie back and wait for the doctor."

"I'll go get Doctor Hadley," said the receptionist.

Aidan and Natalie stood beside Abby.

A few minutes later, Jane and Victoria rushed into the room. "Here's her purse. I gave the receptionist her insurance card."

The door opened again, and Dr. Hadley walked in.

"Abby, what's wrong?"

"Nothing. I just fainted and hit my head. It's no big deal."

"And you vomited, don't forget," added Natalie.

"How could I forget? Pretty soon the whole town will know about it."

"This visit is confidential," said the doctor.

"You know and I know that's not true. There's a whole waiting room full of people out there. It's probably trending on Twitter as we speak. Anything that happens to a Longley is news."

"Why don't you please wait out in the waiting room, all of you," instructed the doctor. "I'll take Abby from here." The room cleared. "How are you feeling?"

"A little weak, I guess. Weird, lightheaded."

"I'm going to order some blood tests to rule some things out." She used the intercom to page her nurse.

When the nurse came in, the doctor instructed, "Please draw some blood from our patient." The nurse walked away for a minute, then steadied Abby's arm and drew several vials of blood. After that she left the room with the samples.

"Abby, has this ever happened to you before? Have you ever fainted like this?" Dr. Hadley asked, as she cleaned and bandaged the wound on Abby's head.

"No."

"Have you been under stress lately?"

"Yes, we just opened a new gallery, and we've

been working for months at a pretty hectic pace."

"What about emotional stress?"

"What do you mean?"

"Is anything going on in your personal life that may have upset you?"

Abby shrugged. "Nothing that would cause me to faint."

"Your blood pressure is normal. That's good." She listened to Abby's heart and asked some additional questions, checking her further. "I'd like to get a urine specimen, if you're up to it. Can you stand on your own?"

"I'm fine, Dr. Hadley. I can pee in a cup, if that's what you mean."

"Call if you need assistance."

Abby rolled her eyes. Dr. Hadley helped her off the table.

"We'll have the preliminary results back in a short while. So, after you leave the sample, just relax here until I come back with some news. You'll have to call my office at the end of the week for the rest of the results."

Dr. Hadley looked at Abby. "Is it possible you're pregnant?"

Abby laughed. "Not likely. You know my history, Dr. Hadley. I've been trying to get pregnant for too many years to count and nothing ever happened. So, no."

"Just had to check, since those symptoms you're describing lead to that conclusion, and there doesn't seem to be anything else wrong with you."

"I'm just run down. Maybe I'm anemic. I'll leave the sample in the bathroom."

Dr. Hadley left the examining room.

Thirty minutes later, Dr. Hadley swept back in.

"Problem solved," she related happily. "It's just what I thought. You're pregnant, Abby. I was fairly sure that was it. You exhibited the classic symptoms."

Abby, already dressed and sitting in the chair in the corner of the room, bolted upright. "That's impossible."

Dr. Hadley put her hand out to keep Abby seated.

"Are you saying you haven't had intercourse?"

"No, that's not what I'm saying. It's just that, like I said, Louis and I tried so hard to have a baby, really tried, and I couldn't get pregnant."

"Well, both the urine test and the blood test came out positive. You are pregnant. I'm going to give you a prescription for prenatal vitamins, and I want you to be sure to schedule a follow-up visit with the receptionist on your way out. And congratulations."

Abby stared straight ahead. The very thing she'd been praying would happen for so long had finally come to pass, but it was too late. What was she going to do?

Abby went out to the waiting room. Jane, Victoria, and Natalie rushed to her side.

"Are you all right?" they asked in unison.

Abby breathed in. "I'm fine. Let me settle my bill. I'll meet you all outside."

As Abby walked out into the sunshine, the day suddenly took on a brilliant hue. The grass seemed greener, the sky bluer, the clouds whiter and wispier. She detected the strong scent of the ocean. Nothing would ever be the same again.

"Could we just make a quick stop at the drugstore?" Abby asked.

"For what?" Natalie said.

"Just a prescription."

Aidan pulled into the drugstore parking lot, and Natalie went into the store with her.

When Abby handed the pharmacist her prescription, Natalie snatched it away.

"Prenatal vitamins? What's going on?"

"What do you think's going on?"

Abby looked around to make sure no one was listening and whispered, "I'm pregnant."

"What?"

"You heard what I said. Let's not talk about this until we get home."

Abby gave the pharmacist her credit card, took the package, and dropped it into her purse.

When they got to the car, Natalie joined Abby in the backseat.

"Okay, what did the doctor say?" Aidan asked.

"Nothing," Abby answered. "I'm perfectly fine."

"Then why did you need a prescription? Natalie, someone needs to tell me what's going on."

"Abby's pregnant."

"Natalie, you have no right to say anything. Aidan, I don't want anyone else to know. *No* one else. Not Tack—especially not Tack. *No one.* Do you understand?"

Aidan started the car. "Tack has a right to know if he's the father. He is the father, isn't he?"

"I haven't been with anyone else. But if I decide to tell Tack, that's my business. Not yours. Promise me you won't say a word."

"I don't like it."

"Aidan, please respect my wishes," Abby pleaded.

"Can I just say congratulations?" Natalie said. "I know how long you've been waiting for this."

"It's just not the right time or place. Not the right man."

Natalie took her friend's hand and squeezed it. "Just the same, I think it's wonderful news."

Aidan grumbled in the front seat. He drove through town and onto Hidden Cove Drive, squinting as the dappled sunlight peeked through the shade of the canopied drive, until they got to Longley House.

"Aidan, watch out for the horse-drawn carriages," Natalie warned as one approached on the opposite side of the road.

"Honey, I've lived here all my life. I've gotten close, but I've never run over any of the tourists or horses."

Abby got out of the car, went up to his front window, and leaned in.

"Aidan, thanks for taking me, and remember—not a word to Tack. Natalie, why don't you and Aidan go out and celebrate your engagement? I'm really happy for the two of you. Have a nice day. I'm going to rest. I'm very tired. Just tell everyone to go on with their plans. Now we know there's nothing wrong with me. I have a lot to think about."

"I hate to leave you alone," Natalie said.

"I'm pregnant, not an invalid."

Abby let herself in the house. The message light was flashing. Tack had called twice, anxious to set up a "meeting." She was so not ready to deal with Tack, not with this new complication. She walked slowly through the gallery and took the elevator up to her room. She removed her clothes and changed into her nightgown, got under the covers, and burst into tears. Were they tears of joy? She didn't know exactly. She'd have to start eating. She was eating for two. But right now, she was bone tired. Too tired to talk. Too tired to think. About the baby. Or about Tack.

Chapter Sixteen

Sunlight crept through the sheer white floor-length curtains. How long had she been asleep? Abby checked her watch on the end table. An entire day. She'd slept the day away. Checking her cell phone, she noted that Tack had left three more messages, each one more frantic than the last. She would have to face him, but not until she was strong enough.

Then another thought occurred to her. Aidan must have told Tack about the pregnancy. She'd asked him to keep her secret, but Aidan was Tack's best friend. That's why he was desperately trying to reach her. He wanted to make this problem go away. Renata had tricked him into marriage with her pregnancy, and Tack thought she was pulling the same stunt. That's something she'd never do.

Abby pushed back the covers, got out of bed, and stared out at the ocean. This town was so peaceful. Why hadn't she realized that before? Why had she always tried to get away from Lobster Cove? Everything she needed was right here. Her friends were here. Her new gallery was here. She was starting a new life. Her hands flew to her stomach. A brand-new life. All the fertility tests, the shots, the doctors' visits… And now she had her miracle. She pushed aside all thoughts of Tack. She'd have to tell him eventually or Aidan would, if he hadn't already. Men were terrible about keeping secrets. And this town was so insular she'd be surprised if the news wasn't already printed in the *Lobster Cove Anchor*. No, she'd have to tell Tack before he found out from someone else. That was the decent thing to do.

Abby stepped into the shower and enjoyed a luxurious soaking. She took the elevator downstairs. There they were. Her three best friends, standing in tandem, arms folded, looks of concern etched on their respective faces.

Victoria was the first to speak. "What are you going to do?"

"I'm going to have a baby," Abby stated.

"I mean about Tack," said Victoria.

"I haven't decided whether or not to tell him."

"Abby, we've discussed it, and we all think you should."

Abby laughed. "You all have decided what's best for me?"

"You can't have this baby alone."

"I won't be alone. I have you, and I don't need Tack. Just because you three have found someone, doesn't mean I have to settle for the first man who comes along."

"Tack is a great guy. Everyone says so."

"It looks like I'm outnumbered. But right now I'm starving. I haven't eaten in a day. So what do we have?"

"A muffin basket with your choice of lemon poppy seed muffins, chocolate chip muffins, zucchini muffins, or blueberry muffins, all of your favorites. And orange juice, which you need to build up your strength. Maybe a glass of milk. We had Chef take away the bacon."

"But I love bacon," Abby protested.

"I know, but you have to think of the baby. Think healthy thoughts. We ate all the bacon before you got downstairs."

"Thanks," Abby said, sarcastically. She sat down at the table and took a blueberry muffin and a glass of orange juice.

"Are you feeling any morning sickness?" Natalie asked.

"Not this morning, but I'm going to carry a package of saltines in my purse, just in case." Abby buttered the muffin and drank the glass of juice with her vitamins.

"So what's on the agenda today?" Abby asked.

"Ethan and I are going to paint all day, up in the loft," said Jane.

"You mean up in your bedroom?"

Jane swallowed a smile.

"Aidan and I are going to take a drive to Bar Harbor. He's going to visit friends while I look for a wedding dress," Natalie announced.

"Do you want some company?" Victoria wanted to know. "Shouldn't your best friends go with you?"

"Right now I'm just going to browse and enjoy the moment. No, you spend some time with Joshua. I know he's leaving tomorrow to deliver the painting. You two don't have much time left together. You need to resolve your feelings."

"I've already resolved them. I've fallen in love with the man. He's so adorable and so formal and—I can't explain it. He just does it for me. I don't know what I'm going to do when he leaves. Emma's flying out this morning to New York. Caleb is taking her to the airport. She had a great time on her date last night.

Caleb, and Tack, also own a restaurant in New York, so he's already made plans to visit her next week. I'm really going to miss her, and I'm going to miss Joshua. But I understand he does important work, and my life is here now. We're geographically incompatible."

"If you're really in love, you can work those things out," Abby assured her.

"I may be in love, but I don't know how Joshua feels. We haven't known each other that long."

"Why don't you spend the day with him and try to work things out?" Abby suggested.

"Meanwhile, what are you going to do, Abby?" Victoria asked.

"Well, the storefront gallery won't open officially for another two weeks, and the gallery at Longley House won't be open again until then, so we have time to regroup and relax for a change. I thought I might sit outside and smell the ocean, get some fresh air. It's been awhile since I just soaked up the sun. Maybe I'll read a book. Maybe I'll go swimming."

"Are you going to call Tack?" Natalie asked pointedly. "He's already called twice this morning."

"Yes, I guess I'll have to face him sooner or later. I don't know if I'll tell him. I'll decide when I hear what he has to say."

Why did life have to be so complicated? If she hadn't gotten pregnant, there would be no need to see Tack again. But Aidan was right. Tack did deserve to know he was going to be a father again. And, whether she wanted to admit it to herself or not, she wanted to see him.

Abby walked into the living room and plopped onto the couch. She picked up her cell phone and dialed

Tack's number. He was probably out on the boat and couldn't get reception, or maybe he was already out with another woman…

He answered on the first ring, startling her. "Tack?"

"Abigail? I've been trying to reach you. Is everything okay?"

"Yes, I got your messages. Have you talked to Aidan?"

"About what? Aidan is otherwise occupied these days, with Natalie. So, no, I haven't talked to him. Why?"

"No reason. I can meet with you today."

"Great. I've got Isabella with me now. We've just come from visiting my father at the nursing home. It really lifted his spirits to see her. I'll drop her off at home and then come over. Do you want to go somewhere?"

"I thought we could just stay here, outside by the ocean, and talk."

"Okay. I'll see you soon. And I wanted to tell you we got the portrait of Isabella. It's wonderful. I've already hung it in the foyer."

"I'm glad."

****

Abby was reading a romance on the couch in the study, her feet propped up on a pillow, when Victoria burst in.

"He's gone!" she cried.

"Who's gone?"

"Joshua."

"I thought you were going to discuss your future."

"We tried, but Joshua says his work is too

important, and he needs to do it in Europe. I explained that my work at the gallery is important to me and that I needed to stay in Lobster Cove."

"Well, Vickie, I'm sure you could come to some sort of compromise, if you love each other."

"That's the problem. He doesn't love me enough. Otherwise, he wouldn't have boarded that plane. You know how *uncompromising* he is. It's either black or white. I either love him enough to move to London or we're through. He made his decision. I kept thinking he would turn back, but he didn't even turn around at the gate. He just got on the plane and flew off."

Vickie sat down on the couch next to Abby.

"I told him I couldn't leave you now. I didn't tell him about your baby. But if I go, who will take care of you? And this gallery means everything to me—you and Natalie and Jane mean everything to me."

Abby put the book down on the coffee table and tried to console her friend.

"Vickie, love is more important. It's a gift. When it comes along, you can't squander it, because it might not come again. We of all people know that. When Joshua arrives home, you can call him and suggest a visit."

"I am not going to make the first move. He left me, and if he cares enough, he'll call me."

****

Tack had been a tiger in a cage all the day before, confined to the house, prowling around, waiting for Abigail's call. And when it finally came the following morning, his heart had stopped for a minute. Was she going to say goodbye forever? Or would she give him a second chance? He hadn't been able to get in touch with Aidan to gauge her state of mind. He didn't dare take out the boat, in case he missed her call. He was moody and hard to be around, he knew.

His mother told him to take a cold shower. "I've never seen you like this, son. If you love this girl, and I think you do, then tell her the truth. She deserves that. If she loves you back, she'll forgive you. And if you don't love her, then let her go." She then took Isabella to a movie to get her out of the house so neither of them had to see him suffer.

Tack had hurried to shower and dress, staring at the phone whenever possible. It was like a watched pot that never boiled. And finally, the call came. Abigail had sounded tired, or was he just imagining that? She had sounded resigned, but resigned to what? He had been deceiving her since they met. How could he explain what he'd done?

She'd asked to meet at her house, which was a bad sign. She was on her own turf. She could easily cut him loose and not have to deal with the consequences: no fighting, no shouting, no begging, no throwing things in a public place. She could just go quietly back to her own life. A life that didn't include him.

Should he bring her flowers? A peace offering of some kind? How did you make up for the sin of attacking the woman you love, and in your car, no less? That was unforgiveable.

And that's what she would say.

He could explain it away as a momentary lapse. But, truthfully, he wasn't sorry he'd done it. He wanted her, and, at that moment, he hadn't been able to help himself.

He had thought of nothing else since that night.

Not only had he attacked her, but he'd been lying to her from the moment they'd met. He could keep second-guessing himself all day.

Or he could just go over there and face her.

Chapter Seventeen

Abby sat still and silent on one of the concrete benches beyond the sculpture garden, by the ocean. She could sit this way for hours watching the lighthouse, listening to the crash of the waves, watching the sea birds swoop and squawk and soar and the sunlight dancing on the water. Staring at the ocean was liberating. All thoughts just disappeared from her head. She had no idea what she was going to tell Tack, or whether she was going to tell him, or how she was going to tell him. How did you spring something like that on a man you barely knew? She'd just have to see where the conversation took them. She closed her eyes.

Someone was gently nudging her shoulder.

"Tack?" Her voice seemed to come from the bottom of a well.

"I think you fell asleep," Tack said. "Thank you for agreeing to see me."

"No problem. I must have dozed off. What is it you wanted to talk to me about?"

Tack took a seat next to Abby.

"Well, since you seem to be all business, I wanted to talk to you about your future. For instance, who is managing your money?"

What a strange question. "Now that Louis is gone, I leave the management of my money to my attorney, Brandon Fairbanks. He has hired a money manager who he guarantees is doing great things with the capital."

"Is that so?" Tack's eyes were bleary, and there was a faint shadow of red on the cheek where she had slapped him a few days before. "In the interest of full disclosure, I thought I'd let you know that *I'm* managing your money. And, in all modesty, I *am* doing great things with your capital."

Abby tensed and raised her fist.

"I hope you're not going to throw something. Especially not another punch." He rubbed his cheek. "I think you may have loosened one of my teeth the other day."

"What else don't I know about you?" Abby demanded, squaring her shoulders and rounding on him.

"Abby, there's something I have to tell you. That I should have told you when we first met."

Abby threw her hands up. More secrets. "What now?"

"It's a good thing you're already sitting down."

Abby and Tack both looked out at the ocean, reluctant to face each other.

"When I ran into you outside of Mariner's Fish Fry, it wasn't the first time I'd seen you."

Abby tilted her head in a question. "I don't understand."

"I mean, yes, it was the first time I'd spoken to you, but I've seen you before, at Louis's funeral and one other time."

"You were at Louis's funeral?"

"Of course, but I was just one of a big crowd of people you weren't really seeing that day, you were so distraught. I wanted to go to you, to comfort you, but I hardly knew you, and it wasn't the time or the place."

"Go to me? What do you mean?"

"From the moment Louis showed me your picture, I knew you were the one, and even before then."

Abby turned to face Tack. "Louis showed you my picture. What picture was that?"

"Oh, it was taken when you two first met in Florence, Italy. Louis and I were always competing—in school for grades, for women, in business, for everything. I wanted what he had. When he got back from Europe, he showed me your picture, the one he took of you at the Uffizi Gallery. With your big brown eyes, your long, flowing strawberry-blonde hair down to your waist, and your sensual features and perfect figure, right in front of the painting *The Birth of Venus.*"

Tack hesitated and then continued with the rest of it. "I was there."

"You were one of Louis's Harvard friends?"

"Yes. He couldn't ditch us fast enough. It's no wonder you didn't remember me. When I first saw you, for a moment I couldn't speak. You were the most beautiful creature I had ever seen. To me, you were the incarnation of a goddess. You looked just like Venus in the picture."

"That's what Louis always used to say. He surmised I might have been related to the artist's model. Anything's possible. I certainly feel a personal connection to that painting."

"Except the model in the painting was nude. You have no idea how many wet dreams I had about you. I'd never been so jealous of Louis in my life, that he got to touch you, to hold you, to taste you, to love you, that you loved him back. You have no idea how many restless nights I spent pining over you, a woman I didn't even know."

Abby blushed.

"I wondered what would have happened if I had seen you first. A few days later, he thought he had lost that picture, and he asked me if I'd seen it. I lied and said I hadn't. But I took the picture out of his wallet. I still have it."

Tack opened his wallet and presented the picture. "A day hasn't gone by that I haven't looked at that picture, at you, and wished you were mine. I've been in love with you—or the idea of you—all this time. And when I heard Louis had died, after my marriage had fallen apart, I was glad I had moved from Boston to Lobster Cove, so I could be near you. A half-baked idea, I know. But love makes you do crazy things. Naturally, when we ran into each other, and you were in my arms, real and alive, I was convinced it was fate. That we were meant to meet. That we were meant to be together. That maybe, somehow, Louis had engineered it—you know, from beyond."

Abby turned over the picture and read Louis's inscription with a catch in her voice. *"To my love, my Venus.* What would Louis say about this, I wonder, about us being here together?"

"I know exactly what he'd say," Tack stated. "What you also don't know is that Louis called me right after he was diagnosed. He knew he was failing, and asked me to take over managing his assets, and he asked me—"

Abby looked into Tack's eyes. "What did he ask

you?"

"He asked me to take care of you when he was gone."

Abby felt faint. Tack had delivered his knockout punch. Was this even possible? "Oh, Tack. Did he really?"

"Yes. It didn't seem fair, and I felt, still feel, so guilty. Louis had everything—great wealth, happiness —and he had you. You were his greatest happiness. He had come to grips with his mortality, but it devastated him to know he was leaving you alone. He paid me the highest compliment. He said he knew he could trust me with you. And only me. He knew how miserable I was, raising Isabella alone. He also knew I was ready to move on, because Renata hadn't been much of a wife to me or a mother to Isabella. But I don't regret marrying her, because she gave me my beautiful daughter. Louis also knew how lonely you'd be. And he thought…that we could make each other happy."

Abby ran her hand through her hair. That was so like Louis, trying to arrange everyone else's happiness, thinking of others before himself. He must have been in such pain, such turmoil, and yet he had thought of this, thought of her welfare.

"So when you pulled away from me that night in the car, well, I thought I was losing you forever, and I couldn't let you go," Tack continued. "Not just for myself, but for Louis. I had already begun to think of you as mine. I'm ashamed of the way I acted. I lost control, because I wanted you so badly. You had just met me, but I've been waiting for you all this time. Waiting for you to love me. I know that's no excuse."

"Were you at our wedding?" Abby asked in a daze.

"There were so many people."

"I couldn't bear to see him marry you. Silly, I know. But I made my excuses." Tack picked up Abby's hand and rubbed the fleshy inside of her palm with his thumb in a circular motion. Abby's insides melted.

He reached over and placed a soft kiss on Abby's lips, then her nose, then her forehead. "This, now, this, is how I imagined it would be between us. Calm and serene. Gentle and slow." He pulled her close, kissed her again, and she dropped her head on his shoulder as they looked out at the ocean.

"I wouldn't blame you for being mad."

"I'm not."

The minutes passed in silence. She supposed they were both thinking of Louis and how he had brought them together. It was her turn to speak.

"Tack, I haven't been completely honest with you, either," Abby began, tightening her grip on Tack's hand for moral support.

"Tell me, sweetheart."

Tack sounded so understanding. Did she have the courage to be honest with him? She had the means to leave Lobster Cove, to have the baby and live somewhere else. Tack never needed to know about the baby. But she didn't want to live anywhere else or with anyone else. Damn the torpedoes. Full speed ahead. What did she have to lose?

"I'm pregnant," Abby began, looking directly at Tack to gauge his reaction.

Tack rocketed out of his seat. "Pregnant? I thought you said you and Louis couldn't—"

"Apparently Louis and I couldn't, but I must still be fertile, because, well, we're going to have a baby."

"Louis was so sorry he couldn't give you the one thing you wanted. He felt like he had failed you."

"He was the only thing I wanted," Abby said wistfully.

"Is it possible you could want me?" Tack got down on his knees and hugged Abigail. "We're going to have a baby!"

"Unexpected, I know."

"It's out of the blue."

"Well, not exactly. We did have sex—unprotected sex. Once, but apparently once is enough." Abby looked out at the ocean as if a solution would suddenly materialize out of the breeze and blow into her mind. "I don't want you to think this means you have to, I mean that we have to. I'm keeping this baby. That's all I ever wanted. But just because we had sex, you're under no obligation to—"

"Obligation? I don't look at it as an obligation. Abigail! My beautiful Abigail..." Tack took Abby into his arms and breathed a sigh of relief. "I'm in love with you, Abigail Adams Longley. And I can't wait to spend the rest of my life with you. From the moment I saw you on the pier, I wanted to be with you, every day, every minute, every second. I couldn't bear it when we were apart."

"Tack." Abby could hardly breathe. She could actually feel her heart kicking out of her chest, lining up at the starting gate, ready to run a marathon. She clung to him. The waterworks were back, and she couldn't stop them.

Tack pulled away. "You're crying." Tack wiped away her tears.

"I'm happy, Tack. I've wanted a baby for a long

time. I wanted a baby with Louis, but Louis is gone. I can do this on my own."

"I don't have any doubt about that. But I want to be there for you, for our baby. I want you in my life more than anything in the world. Now that I'm down on bended knee, I may as well do this right," Tack said, clasping Abigail's hands. "Abigail Adams Longley, will you marry me?"

Abby leaned her head onto Tack's forehead. Suddenly, the solution was simple. She didn't have to think twice. "Yes, I'll marry you."

Abigail was still wearing the engagement ring Louis had given her. Tack rubbed his finger over it. "I can afford a ring, you know, which will mean you'll have to take this one off."

Abby fingered Louis's ring. She'd never wanted to part with it. But she'd made a commitment to Tack, and it was time to let go of the past. Abby removed Louis's ring and put it in her pocket.

"I wish I had come prepared, but I thought there was a chance you might throw me out on my ass," Tack admitted.

Abby laughed. "That was a distinct possibility."

"I come from a long line of whaling captains, although there was one black sheep in the family, a pirate. And this pirate salvaged a Spanish galleon in the Adriatic and recovered a large emerald—the Garrity emerald. It's priceless. And, some say, cursed. But since I met you, my luck has changed. And there is no one I know more worthy to wear it."

"I'd be honored," Abby said.

"I'm going to go right to the bank for it and take it to Jewels of the Sea to have it cleaned and sized."

"And you no doubt own Jewels of the Sea."

"I'm an investor."

"Then I think we should go to your house and tell Isabella together."

"She is going to go mad with joy," Tack said. "She loves you, you know, almost as much as I do."

"And I love her."

"And what about me? How do you feel about me?"

"Tack, I'll be honest with you. I wasn't looking for love. I never thought I would find it again, but I fell in love with you. I fought it. I felt guilty for being this happy, because of Louis. But Louis wanted this for us. He arranged it. I think that's a sign. So the answer is yes, I love you, Tack."

"Abigail, I will devote the rest of my life to making you happy. I promise you that."

"Where will we live?"

"I'll build you a new house. A house of our own, just for our family. I have just the spot in mind. We'll go up there today and take a look at it, see if it meets your approval. Then we'll have Aidan draw up some plans. Would you like that?"

"Tack, it sounds wonderful."

"I want to get married as soon as possible. We can have the wedding here at the gallery, just outside in the garden. It will be a beautiful backdrop."

"That's a fantastic idea. Tack, I hope I can make you happy."

"How can you doubt that? Now let's go tell Isabella."

"And I've got to tell my friends. They won't be surprised. I think they knew I was in love with you, before I knew myself."

"So did my mother. And there's another Garrity I want you to meet. My pop. I told him I was going to marry you."

"The bride is always the last to know."

Epilogue

His bride was a vision, in a Monique Lhuillier blush georgette, strapless, sweetheart lace gown with white silk embroidered tulle overlap and Watteau train. Her three bridesmaids—Natalie, Victoria, and Jane—wore blush shirred chiffon gowns with lace yokes. Isabella, her maid of honor, wore a blush floor-length dress with an outer layer of organza added to a classic satin base, a fitted, sleeveless bodice, and a slightly higher-than-natural waist. And no tutu! Abigail and Isabella—his Venus and their princess—wore matching Longley heirloom diamond tiaras. And, of course, Abigail wore the priceless Garrity emerald that sparkled in the afternoon sunlight but didn't come close to outshining Abigail.

And the best thing was that Abby had ordered all the gowns from Wedded Bliss, which he also owned an interest in. He'd loaned proprietor Kelly Andrews the money to start her business. Now it was a one-stop shop to buy anything wedding-related. Abigail had also hired Kelly to be her wedding planner. She was making an effort to reach out and make friends in the community. Lobster Cove was becoming her real home.

What did he remember about that day? The weather cooperated. It was a garden wedding at Longley House, overlooking the ocean and the lighthouse, followed by an elegant reception at the

Venus Gallery, catered by the Crow's Nest, of course. The orchestra was warming up inside, the tables and chairs were set up, the bar stocked and staffed. The flowers from the Longley garden were arranged to complement the décor. The good Longley china service was taken out of storage. There were some Garrity touches, as well, such as his mother's white Celtic Irish linen damask tablecloth and silver service.

Over the next few months, there were to be three more weddings. His and Abigail's was followed by Aidan and Natalie's, then Jane and Ethan's, and they were all going to sail over on a transatlantic cruise to celebrate the wedding of Victoria and Joshua. After a month apart from Victoria, Joshua had realized he couldn't live without her, and he flew back to Lobster Cove to propose. Following the wedding in London, the couples, who had postponed their honeymoons to launch the gallery, were free to honeymoon anywhere they chose in Europe. He and his bride had chosen the romantic venue of Lake Como, Italy. Jane and Ethan were going on a painting holiday in Paris. Aidan and Natalie had decided to take a river cruise along the Seine.

Ethan and Jane would live at Longley House. Joshua and Victoria would make their home in London, but Vickie had decided she could handle the marketing and Web business from there, with frequent trips to Lobster Cove, and she'd be free to go on buying trips for the gallery or join Abby when she traveled overseas to shop for the gallery. She felt more comfortable about her decision because Val McKinley, the woman who had saved the little boy from being run over by a moving trolley, had reapplied and was hired to manage the gallery two days a week. She was extremely efficient, and her presence had given Vickie a lot more flexibility. In fact, she was having quite an influence on Abby. His bride preferred European art, while Val opened up new doors by convincing her to include in the gallery a wider variety of modern artists from both the Western Hemisphere and Asia.

He had never seen Isabella happier. She finally had the mother she deserved. And she was looking forward to meeting her new little sister or brother. He and Abigail had decided to get married quickly, not just because of the baby—Abby's baby bump was hardly showing—but because he couldn't live without her for one more minute. He hoped they would be blessed with a houseful of children.

They would live at Longley House until their dream home was built. Aidan had already drawn up the plans.

But what he remembered most about his wedding day was that moment when Abigail walked down the aisle toward him. He had to catch his breath because she was heart-stoppingly beautiful. More beautiful than Venus. The most beautiful woman he had ever seen or ever would see. The photographer could not possibly capture her elusive smile or the look of joy on her face as she placed her delicate hand in his—and her trust in him. "Finally" was what he was thinking. Finally, she was his. At last, they would be together. After all the heartbreak and tragedy, their destinies would be intertwined. He didn't know what he'd done to deserve her, but he was going to spend the rest of his life making her happy she had chosen him.

But what he was looking forward to most was

loving Abigail, finally being able to show her how much she meant to him, what a gift she was, how grateful he was that she had come into his and Isabella's lives.

When they danced their first dance together, he'd held her in his arms and never wanted to let her go.

"I can't wait until we're alone. I want to show you how much I love you, how much I treasure you."

Abby blushed. Of course they had been alone together before the wedding. They couldn't stay away from each other. When they came together alone at night, it was like an explosion of thunder and lightning in the night sky, and afterwards like a blanket of gentle rain. He wanted to show her his tender side. She was everything to him. His Abigail. His Venus.